I0658843

THE OLD BLOCK

THE OLD BLOCK

A Novel

Mark Scott Piper

The Old Block

Copyright © 2020 Mark Scott Piper

All rights reserved

ISBN: 978-1-7355044-0-7

This is a work of fiction. Names, characters, businesses, places, events, locales, and incidents are either the products of the author's imagination or used in a fictitious manner. Any resemblance to actual persons, living or dead, or actual events is purely coincidental.

This book may not be reproduced, transmitted, or stored in whole or in part by any means, including graphic, electronic, or mechanical without the express written consent of the publisher except in the case if brief quotations embodied in critical articles and reviews.

BLUE ZEBRA PRESS

Cover Design: Nick Castle Design
Cover Photo: shutterstock.com
Author Photo © 2019 Karen Amber Miller. All rights reserved – used with permission.

PRINTED IN THE UNITED STATES OF AMERICA

Dedication

To Frank Newton "Pat" Piper, who taught me by example
how to be the best father I could be.
I will always miss you, Dad.

Acknowledgments

Ultimately, I am responsible for every word in this novel, but I didn't get it to this point alone. Over the years spent on writing, rewriting, editing and re-editing I received plenty of input and suggestions from writers and friends who helped make this novel what it has become.

I'll be forever indebted to my editor Amber Miller. Her suggestions managed to open my eyes and keep me on the right track. She has made me a better writer.

Donna Banta provided invaluable help polishing the final draft. Donna, Ruth Schuler, and Jon Shearer—faithful members of our longstanding critique group and talented writers all—have critiqued the early versions of the novel and demonstrated ongoing support, indispensable suggestions, and the patience of saints.

A special thanks to the members of The Internet Writing Workshop, who stayed the course through several months of weekly online submissions. Every writer needs a benevolent editor, and I'm lucky enough to have had several.

Beth Partin's thorough and insightful proofreading of the finished manuscript was both crucial and humbling. Any inadvertent errors in the manuscript are mine.

My children—Robyn, Michelle, Colin, and Courtney—continue to encourage me to follow my dream. You are my legacy.

Chapter 1

May 2012

I splashed cold water on my face to shock some life into it. I should be doing better than this. Over a month since the funeral, and I still wasn't getting much sleep. I glanced at my reflection, eased out a sigh. Every time I looked in a mirror I saw Dad looking back at me. Easy enough to see why: same dark eyes, same jawline, same smile. A smile that didn't come easily for me these days. At least I didn't break into tears this time.

I ran a palm over my cheek. I'd either have to shave or commit to growing a beard. I flicked on the Norelco and started in on my six-day-old stubble. The buzz of the razor wasn't loud enough to block out the voices that still wouldn't leave me alone.

◆ ◆ ◆

The clamor of a hundred simultaneous conversations overwhelms me at the post-funeral gathering in the Shoat Valley Presbyterian Church. The whole town has turned out.

The barrage never lets up. Everyone feels compelled to corner me, pay their respects, share their fond memories of Jim Castle—his kindness, his gentle way with people, his humility, his willingness to step in and help. As if I somehow didn't already know what he was like.

Mary Ellen Camp, our mayor, pumps my hand with her two-handed candidate's grip. "Nick, your dad's smile always lit up the room. He will be missed."

Charley Hanson, the town pharmacist and Dad's frequent golf partner, leans in close to remind me: "Jim Castle was truly an honest man. Might be the only guy I know who never once cheated at golf." I reward his hearty guffaw with a forced smile.

Mom's sister, Eloise, sincere as always, drunk as always, covers me with sloppy kisses and tells me, "Your dad was one of a kind. He could make anyone feel special ... even those of us who weren't. I'll never forget the time I'd had too much to drink, and I started to sound off about how life wasn't fair and ..."

I tune her out. I've heard that story so often, it's embedded in my brain.

◆　◆　◆

Okay, they were going to miss him. I got that. But now that gathering and those songs of praise were long gone. Those well-wishers had moved on as if nothing had happened. Their day-to-day activities shifted back to normal. Mine wouldn't. My mentor, my role model, my best friend ... my *dad* was dead. And now, my life had a cavernous void in the middle of it that would never be filled.

The Old Block

Dad and I did everything together. I was his shadow. For my whole life, the adults in Shoat Valley have referred to me as "Little Jim," "a chip off the old block," "the apple of his dad's eye," or "a spittin' image of the old man." Some still applied, but tired clichés couldn't begin to describe our relationship.

As a young child, I was a fixture at Dad's side at our family bookstore, Book Castle, and I tagged along while he ran errands. Even when I was only three or four, Dad would let me "help" by carrying packages back to the car, including some that were probably too big or awkward to trust me with. A proud moment. When I was older, I realized he most likely secretly spotted me the whole way, but he never let me know that.

I still remember, early on—I must have been five or six—my first Little League game. I'd failed miserably that day. I missed a couple of grounders, made a bad throw, and my performance at the plate should have earned me the nickname "Whiff." On the way home in the car, I stared straight ahead trying to hold back tears.

Dad pulled over to the side of the road and stopped the car. After a moment, he laid his hand on my shoulder. "Don't be so hard on yourself, Nick. It takes time to master this game."

I looked over at him, my lower lip quivering my response.

He pulled me into a hug. "You've got to remember, Kiddo, baseball is a game of failure." He ruffled my hair. "The best hitters in the big leagues average only three hits for every ten at-bats."

"Wait. So, they fail seven out of ten times? Really?"

"Yep. But don't worry, you've got the skills. You just need some help developing them."

"What does that mean?" I wiped away the remnants of tears with my sleeve.

"Means you need some personal instruction." He chuckled. "And you're in luck. I know just the guy who can do it." He threw his hands out to the side, grinned.

We both knew who he was referring to.

When we got home, he took me out to the backyard and showed me the basics of playing the game. We laughed, kidded around, had a lot of fun. No pressure, no disappointment. It was just the two of us. And we were out there nearly every day for weeks.

He taught me plenty of skills—how to place my feet in the batter's box, how to generate power when I swung, all that stuff. But most of all he taught me how to have fun playing the game. It was a lesson in baseball and in life that I've tried to hang on to ever since.

I've never been as close to anyone in my life. Guess that's why it's been so hard for me to let go. Even at Sonoma State, I regularly Skyped with my parents, most often Dad on Book Castle's computer. And when I returned to Shoat Valley with a degree, we picked up right where we left off. My degree was in English, which, if nothing else, made me a good candidate to run a bookstore someday. But Dad made sure I thought my career options through. Even an English major has some choices. I'm sure he knew all I really wanted to do was follow in his footsteps. Same as I always had.

But now, his footsteps were gone forever, and I wasn't sure what that meant for me. Everything I did, everything I believed in, everything I hoped to *become* was a reflection of Dad. Being Jim Castle's son *defined* me—like being Batman's sidekick defined Robin. And now? Well, now it didn't. Robin without Batman was just some weirdo in tights waiting for instructions.

◆ ◆ ◆

I stepped out of my studio apartment above Book Castle and descended the stairs to the back door of the bookstore. Once inside, I took care of all the opening chores: turned on the lights, checked the thermostat, started up the coffee maker and espresso machine, unlocked the big double door. I sat down at the store's old wooden desk—the one Dad and I refinished when I was twelve—and powered up the computer. Of the six file icons on the screen, the one labeled DAD-OBIT stared back at me, daring me to click it, but I didn't have to. I knew it by heart. I'd written it for the local newspapers following a standard formula.

The highlights: James Franklin Castle. Succumbed to prostate cancer at sixty-two. Gone too soon. Loving husband and father, friend to all he met, owner of the popular Book Castle bookstore, model citizen, honored three times for his community service, named Shoat Valley's 1998 Citizen of the Year. Survived by Katherine Elaine Castle, his wife of twenty-seven years, and two grown children, Shelby Anne Castle, twenty-one, and me, Nicolas James Castle, twenty-four. I'd covered all the bases, but an obituary can only scratch the surface of a man's life. Especially this man.

The obit appeared in the *Shoat Valley Register* over a month ago, and the icon had been sitting on the computer desktop long enough. Seeing it every day wasn't helping me cope. Time to stash it away on the hard drive. The battery on the wireless mouse, however, had died overnight. The irony didn't escape me.

I took some deep breaths, waiting for the tightness in my chest to subside. Then, rummaging around in the top desk drawer for the charger, I spied the corner of a white envelope at the back. Dad had given it to me almost two years ago when the doctors first slammed us with the diagnosis of inoperable prostate cancer.

◆　◆　◆

He and I were sitting on the couch about a week after the doctors had given us the devastating news. We were pretending to watch some documentary about endangered species. I wasn't paying attention. My mind was still trying to process what life was going to be like … without Dad.

"Jesus, this is too depressing." He clicked off the television and stood. "Follow me." He tilted his head toward the kitchen. "I've *got* something for you."

I trailed behind him through the kitchen into the garage. He rummaged around on his tool bench, making me think he was going to bequeath me something both practical and manly, like a power saw. But when he straightened back up, he was holding a standard white mailing envelope. My name was written on the front.

He held the envelope out to me, and I took hold of it, but he didn't let it go.

He pulled it, and me, toward him and leaned closer. "Nick, you have to promise me something … and you absolutely have to *keep* that promise."

"Of course, Dad. Anything. You can count on me."

6

He looked me in the eye. "Yeah, I know. I need you to stash this away somewhere private." He let go of the envelope. "Promise me you won't open this until after I'm deceased."

I winced. "But you're going to be around … for a while. The doctors say you have—"

"Promise me."

I'd never seen such pain in his eyes.

"Okay, I promise I won't open this envelope until after you're … gone." I looked away. That whole concept left a lump in my throat I couldn't quite swallow. The promise didn't matter much anyway, since I still refused to accept that he might not make it.

Dad wrapped his arms around me and held tight. We didn't need words.

I can still feel that hug.

♦ ♦ ♦

Once I'd plugged the charger into the mouse, I headed over to the espresso machine, pulled a couple of shots, and made myself a double latte. Through all the chaos of chemotherapy, radiation, blood-count scares, and watching, helpless, as the disease devoured Dad from the inside more each day, I hadn't even thought about that envelope. But now? Time to open it. Now, Dad was … gone. Forever. I sucked in a ragged breath, wiped my nose with the back of my hand, and set my cup on the desk. Slipping the envelope from the drawer, I placed it in front of me. I sipped my latte; somehow it seemed to soothe my sore, scratchy throat.

I took great care not to damage the contents as I removed a sheet of paper, folded in thirds to fit into the envelope. The sheet was *blank*. No letter, no note, no life-affirming instructions. Just a single small key taped inside the folded sheet. Scrawled on its tag was "SVS #12." I knew immediately what it was. A key to a storage locker at Shoat Valley Storage. Book Castle rented two storerooms there—twenty-seven and twenty-eight—where we kept inventory, shelving, and miscellaneous other crap. I'd been to those lockers more times than I could count. But I knew nothing about number twelve. Why would Dad be so secretive about that one? An icy wave rushed through me. A storage locker could hold *anything*.

Our part-timer, Janey Grimes, would be in at ten. Mom was due at noon. That's when I could be spared. And that's when I'd be able to find the answer.

It promised to be a long morning.

Chapter 2

Ralphie Stumple nodded a greeting from his regular spot behind the manager's desk at Shoat Valley Storage. I waved and turned down the hallway. Number twelve looked to be identical to our other ten-by-ten storage units. But its old, corroded padlock required several tries before it screeched open, protesting the intrusion.

The musty, acrid smell that slapped me in the face made my eyes water. Jesus, this place was supposed to be climate controlled. And the light switch didn't work. I needed to have a word with Stumple about this. Even in the glow of the fluorescent hallway lights, the dark cavern looked empty. It made no sense. Why would Dad give me a key to an empty storage locker? Did he change his mind?

Then I noticed it. A beat-up, brown leather satchel leaning against the wall just inside the door. I reached down and cradled it with both hands. The well-worn strap looked too frayed to support anything. One more quick survey of the locker confirmed my earlier assessment. Empty. I knew how it felt.

I stepped into the well-lit hallway, lifted the bag's stained and scratched flap, and extracted a large manila envelope. No writing on the outside. Despite being taped shut, it was stuffed so full it seemed ready to burst at the seams. When I slit open the top with my pocketknife and eased the pressure on the contents, I could have sworn I heard a sigh of relief. I carefully wriggled the top sheet free just far enough to recognize Dad's handwriting on the yellowed notebook paper, the kind we used in grade school. Was this some sort of journal?

No, wait. Dad once told me he'd hoped to write a novel someday. Could this be a draft of that novel? My heart pounded against my rib cage like a heavy-metal drummer. I was about to become the first person to read whatever this turned out to be.

Dad had always been my first reader. He'd read every short story I ever wrote, only one of which was ever published, and that one appeared in the *Sonoma State Star*, the student-run newspaper. My degree was in English, but I'd taken a few creative writing courses along the way. I didn't have the guts to commit fully to going for a fine arts degree.

Over time, I'd collected an impressive list of email rejections from literary journals. Each felt like a gut punch; each bit off a chunk of my self-esteem. Dad was more hopeful. I can still hear our conversation as if it had happened this morning, still feel his arm around my shoulders.

It was a Thursday afternoon well before Dad got sick. Just the two of us in the bookstore. I punched up the email on my phone and showed him my latest form rejection. "I'm starting to think I'll never make it as a writer. Maybe I'm just not good enough."

He stared at me until I could meet his eyes. "Nick, it's only one person's opinion. A person who doesn't even know you. Doesn't mean no one else wants to read your stuff."

"I *wish*."

"Quit *now*, and you'll never know. Look, you have a lot of talent, but the truth is, talent is only one leg of the stool. Sometimes tenacity ... *heart* is just as important as skill."

"Maybe, but sooner or later you have to wake up, realize you just aren't gonna make it."

Dad tilted his head to the side, watched me. "You're right. You might not. But you'll never know unless you give it your best shot." He shut his eyes tight, opened them. "When I was young, I had dreams of becoming a novelist someday ... but my life took a different turn. Maybe I wouldn't have been any good at it, but now I'll never know. Still bothers me from time to time."

I gave him a playful punch on the shoulder. "But you have to admit you've made a pretty good life despite the fact you're *selling* books instead of writing them. Maybe things turned out better for you *because* you never became a famous author."

Dad chuckled. "Yeah, you're probably right. I couldn't ask for a better life than the one I've had with you guys. But that doesn't mean I have no regrets." His eyes glazed over.

I bided my time. I never interrupted him when he drifted off like this.

Dad turned back to me with a sad-serious expression. "Nick, promise me one thing."

"Sure, Dad, anything."

"When you find something … or more importantly, some*one* you love, I mean *really* love, promise me you won't walk away." He looked me in the eye, pointed a finger at my chest. "Because if you do, you might blow the last chance you'll ever have at real happiness."

♦　♦　♦

At the time, I took this to be good, but pretty generic advice—it was hardly revolutionary wisdom. I mean, I knew how deeply he loved Mom. As I recalled that conversation now, though, those words seemed to take on a special significance. Maybe because he and I would never have a moment like that again.

I settled the bulging manila envelope back into the satchel and hid it all under my jacket. I didn't know what this was, but I did know it was meant for my eyes only. It was something Dad wanted to share with me. Just me. It gave me goosebumps.

Back in the bookstore, I told Mom I wasn't feeling well. And as I knew she would, she told me to take the rest of the day off.

"I'll be okay. I'm just going to sleep it off. See you tomorrow." If I didn't tell her that, she'd be up to check on me regularly.

I escaped out the back door of Book Castle, hurried up the stairs to my studio apartment, set the package on the desk, and flicked on the lamp. My hands wouldn't stop trembling, I felt lightheaded. Had I come down with something for real? A couple of deep, calming breaths helped. I sat down at the desk and slit open the side of the overstuffed envelope enough to ease out the pages. How did Dad ever get so many in there in the

12

first place? Askew, on top of the stack, was a half-page note in Dad's bold hand:

> "Nick, when you read the contents of this envelope, you will have a decision to make. Whatever you decide to do will be the right thing. This note is my last chance to tell you that I still love you all as much as any man could ever love his family. Dad."

A chill raced through me. Dad's voice from the afterlife. I wiped my eyes with my sleeve. I wasn't sure I could handle this. Not yet.

When I shuffled through the pages, I discovered the handwritten manuscript had been organized into twenty-five short sections, each indicated by a Roman numeral. Here and there words were crossed out and others inserted, as if Dad had edited on the fly.

Whatever this was, one thing was clear. I was the only person Dad trusted with it.

I wiped my moist palms on the front of my shirt, eased out a ragged breath, and picked up the top page.

Chapter 3

I

Braden Delaney came from money. He always had everything he wanted. Maybe that explained some of it.

His parents were disappointed when he showed no interest in Yale, their alma mater. They would have settled for any Ivy League school. Instead, he applied to a small liberal arts college, Carlyle University, in the tiny town of Sinclair, Washington, clear across the country from his home in Waltham, Massachusetts. Those three thousand miles were one of the main reasons he chose it.

In the spring of 1970, he'd just turned twenty, a sophomore—intelligent, athletic, and popular. Braden maintained a B+ average, and this season he was the starting third baseman for the Carlyle Coyotes. He and the team were having a good year.

Braden and his girlfriend, Cheryl Stevens, were rarely apart. He was taken with her from their first day in freshman English. She was smart, confident, funny, and absolutely beautiful. Even so, it was Cheryl who made the initial contact, because, as she told him, "I was "tired of waiting for you to work up the nerve to ask me out."

Now, after almost a year of dating, everyone could see they were genuinely in love. Everyone except Cheryl's parents, who told her they would disown her if she continued to see Braden, whom they considered to be inappropriate for a young woman studying to become a concert pianist. Braden and Cheryl knew there was more to it than that. Whatever their motivation, Cheryl's parents demanded she break it off with Braden immediately. It was the wrong threat to make to a headstrong young woman like Cheryl Stevens. She chose her heart, and her parents made good on their threat. They cut her off financially and ceased all communication. Braden could tell she was hurt more than she let on, but she rarely ever spoke of her parents again.

Braden and Cheryl were soon caught up in rallies, sit-ins, and class boycotts, as student protests against U.S. involvement in the Vietnam War gained momentum on campuses all across the nation in 1970. Even at a small school like Carlyle, nearly half of the students joined in anti-war protests. Cheryl and Braden watched the news, dumbfounded, as National Guard troops opened fire on student protesters at Kent State—killing four and wounding nine. Braden and Cheryl were caught by surprise. No one expected an overreaction like that to a peaceful protest, not even from the military.

They ramped up their anti-war activity at Carlyle as part of the nationwide reaction to the "Kent State Massacre." With Braden at her side, Cheryl made impassioned speeches that helped convince others at Carlyle to join a nationwide student strike.

Then the National Guard bayoneted eleven student protestors at the University of New Mexico. Shortly after that, two students were killed and twelve more wounded by police at an anti-war rally at Jackson State. The Associated Press ran a picture of the huge sign hung outside a dorm at New York University: "They Can't Kill

Us All." That became a rallying cry for Braden and Cheryl. Protests increased among students and a good portion of faculty members all across the country. Soon, the accelerating avalanche of protests led most colleges, including Carlyle, to suspend classes for the rest of the term. The battle lines were drawn. It was clear to college students everywhere that it was us against them.

Braden and Cheryl met in secret with eight like-minded students and faculty and hatched a plan to make a major anti-war statement. They wanted to show the world that, even at a small school like Carlyle, students were a force to be reckoned with.

One of the people at the meeting wasn't a student. He went by "Cobra" and claimed to be a member of the infamous Weather Underground. There were whispers, but nobody was sure why he showed up at Carlyle or how he found out about the meeting. These weren't questions worth pursuing. What mattered was the movement.

The group was in the middle of a seemingly endless discussion about procedure and strategy, when Braden stood and called a halt. He argued for an act of protest that couldn't be shoved aside by the news media. He

17

argued that, since the National Guard wielded military tactics against students, they needed to make a statement in kind here at Carlyle. Nothing short of bombing Patton Hall, Carlyle's ROTC building, would make a big enough impression. He pleaded, "It would be symbolic … and it would be *real*."

Cobra stood to join Braden. "I agree. The ROTC building is the perfect target for lots of reasons. And even in a small burg like Sinclair, we'll have no trouble finding everything we need to construct a pipe bomb powerful enough to do some major damage."

Some in the room looked skeptical.

Cobra held up his hands. "Look, I have plenty of experience with pipe bombs. Only two possible issues: you have to be diligent and extra cautious when you're making the bomb … and whoever places the device inside the building has to be fast enough to put plenty of distance between him and the explosion." He looked at Braden. "What we need is an athlete."

Braden nodded. "Okay, I get it. I'll do it."

At precisely 9:00 p.m. the next Friday, Cheryl Stevens began a rousing anti-war speech from the front steps of the Administration Building. Soon the mantra, "No more war!" gained momentum until more than a hundred protestors were chanting in unison. That was Braden's signal.

Dressed all in black, including a ski mask and gloves, Braden made his way along the side of Patton Hall two blocks from the rally. He carried a nondescript black backpack containing the partially constructed pipe bomb; all but two wires were connected. Using the boisterous crowd for cover, Braden smashed out a window at the back of the building and climbed inside. He saw no one, and nobody responded when he shouted, "Help! We need to help the campus police. There's a riot outside." He yelled twice more and then made a quick check of every office in the single-story building until he was satisfied they were empty.

Braden connected the remaining two wires from the pipe to the alarm-clock timer and set it for thirty seconds. Then he wedged the bomb in place, slid back out the window, and bolted toward the football stadium about a hundred yards away. Braden dove for cover just as the loudest explosion he'd ever heard ripped open the night. Within minutes flames completely engulfed Patton Hall.

He stuffed the black sweatshirt into a campus clothes-drive box, buried the ski mask and each of the gloves in separate garbage cans, and crouched down in the shadows to wait. Ten minutes after the blast, Braden joined Cheryl amid the raucous crowd now gathering near the fire. Several of the protestors cheered with each new burst of flame. The campus police, red-faced and huffing, tried their best to move people away from the fire as the first sirens wailed in the distance.

Braden had done it. He'd shown the power elite that, even at Carlyle, students weren't about to back down.

II

By Saturday afternoon, news of the explosion at Carlyle had reached the national media. The Sinclair Fire Department immediately identified the explosion and fire as arson. A military investigative team was sent to campus, and the media claimed that Washington State National Guard troops and FBI special agents were on their way. There were no suspects mentioned yet, but law enforcement officials and Carlyle's administration vowed to "make an all-out effort to apprehend and punish to the full extent of the law whoever was responsible for this cowardly act of violence."

As the de facto leaders of the campus radical faction, Braden and Cheryl were questioned right away. The investigation soon heated up, and they both knew authorities were breathing down Braden's neck. Soon enough someone would rat him out. He had to disappear. And fast.

He withdrew the remaining six thousand dollars of the money his parents had sent to cover tuition and expenses for the school year. He gassed up his silver Datsun 240Z and parked it about a half mile from Cheryl's house.

Vancouver, Canada, was less than a three-hour drive. He could be there before the authorities even knew he was gone. Once there, he could easily get lost in the growing population of American draft dodgers and expatriates.

Going without Cheryl would be difficult for them both, but Braden knew what he had to do.

Cheryl had her own plan. Her jaw set, she announced, "I'm going with you. I don't want to take the chance of losing you."

Braden held her at arm's length and shook his head. "Baby, we've been through this. I don't want to leave you either, but you know how dangerous it'll be out there on the run."

Cheryl fought back tears. "I don't *care* how dangerous it is. My place is with you."

"Cheryl, I love you too much to put you at risk. Besides, it'll be a hell of a lot more difficult for two people to keep a low profile."

She settled into his embrace, trembling against him, and whispered, "I've already lost the love of my parents. I don't know if I can survive without you."

He hugged her tight. "Of course you can." He released her and peered into her captivating deep brown eyes. "Baby, you'll never lose my love. And you're the strongest woman I know. You *have* to stay. We both know that if you take off now, the movement here won't last a week. You have to keep the protests going. Without your voice, no one will hear our message."

"But how will I know you're … all right?" She fought back tears.

"I'll contact you as soon as I find a safe way to do it. But the feds already know you're my girlfriend, and once I'm gone, they'll be watching your every move. They'll probably monitor your phone and your mail."

Cheryl's mouth quivered. "Promise me you'll try to at least let me know you're alive?" She squeezed her eyes shut, tears spilling down her cheeks.

"I promise. Trust me, I'll miss you every day I'm away from you."

But Braden knew the FBI and the military were tenacious. Cheryl would only be safe if he didn't contact her for a long time. Maybe ever.

Her desperate expression told him she understood the truth beneath the promise. "Oh, Braden, I … we're never going to see each other again, are we?"

"I'll be gone for a while is all. I'll never forget you. Once things settle down, I'll try to send for you. You already know how I feel. You'll *always* be in my heart and my dreams."

Cheryl took his face in her hands and kissed him with such longing and emotion it caught him by surprise. Braden responded in kind, and soon they collapsed onto the bed and shared the most fiercely passionate night they'd ever experienced.

Just before dawn, he stuffed his backpack with a few clothes, the cash, and all the nonperishables he could get his hands on. Braden didn't look back, but he could feel Cheryl watching him disappear into the cold, early morning mist.

◆ ◆ ◆

I stretched my legs under the desk and took in a deep breath. Wow! Exciting stuff. It was more than just an interesting story to me, though. Reading Dad's words was an emotional experience—it was as if I could *hear* him telling me the story. I eased away from my desk and took the five steps to my tiny kitchenette, where I filled the coffee maker and flicked the switch. I was going to be here a while.

Chapter 4

III

Just as Braden reached his car, Cobra emerged from the shadows. To Braden, Cobra's long dark hair and full black beard made him look a little too much like Rasputin. Could have been a delusion brought on by anxiety. "Someone turned on you, man. They know you did the ROTC building, and the feds are closing down the area fast. You gotta *move*."

Braden clutched his backpack to his chest and swallowed hard. "I'll be in Canada in a few hours."

"Bad idea." Cobra snickered. "Come on, man, that's the most obvious escape route. Get real. The fuzz is probably at the border already. You better head south. We have some people who'll let you hide out for a few days."

"We?"

Cobra nudged Braden toward the 240Z. "I'll explain on the way."

Once they were on the road, Cobra pulled a map from his jacket pocket. "Stay off the main highway, take I-82 south and then cut through the Yakama Indian Reservation on 97, and we can cross the Columbia into Oregon. We have a place near Wasco just over the border."

Braden glanced over at Cobra. "Okay, we're on the way. Now, who the hell is *we*?"

Cobra laughed. "I told you. I'm with the Weather Underground. I've been scouting campuses in the Northwest to recruit other radical students to join us."

Braden winced. "You guys are known for violent protests. People have been killed."

"Yeah, sometimes there are casualties. But this is war."

"Sorry, man." Braden shook his head. "Being vocal, protesting, resisting … I'm fine with all that. But I'm not getting involved in any fuckin' killings."

"Chill, dude. Not asking you to do anything you don't want to do. I'm just sayin' we have a network of safe houses and hideouts, and I can introduce you to people who'll help you stay under the radar ... and that's *exactly* what you need right now. Trust me, man, I'm just tryin' to help you out here."

The only glitch in the plan was that they were stopped when they drove onto Yakama reservation lands. The reservation cop who pulled them over claimed they were speeding. But after a short discussion, he decided to take the hundred dollars Braden offered him, rather than deal with all the paperwork he'd have to fill out if he wrote them a speeding ticket. They promised the cop they'd follow the posted limits and wouldn't be stopping anywhere on the rez.

When they arrived at the safe house, a couple of miles west of Wasco, Oregon, Braden pulled into the gravel driveway next to an old VW bus. Turned out the bus belonged to a mellow hippie couple, who introduced themselves as Joshua and Marigold. They didn't ask him his name or any other questions, and he didn't offer any information. They were heading off to Sadie's Farm, a commune outside Medford, near the California border. The bus was packed and ready to go.

"Gonna have to ditch the Z, man," Cobra said.

"What? Why would I want—"

"Get real, dude, every cop in the Northwest is already looking for it. Now that they know you've split you won't get ten miles in that car."

"I don't know if—"

"Don't worry. I'll take care of the Z for you. Right now, you gotta get your ass moving." He waved his hand toward the Volkswagen.

"Okay, I get it. A donation to the cause," I said.

Cobra smirked. "More like a fee for helpin' you escape and gettin' you a place to hide out."

"Right." Braden grabbed his backpack from the back seat, tossed Cobra his keys, and climbed aboard the bus. It was the last he heard of Cobra or his 240Z.

Joshua and Marigold already knew he was on the run from the feds and that he'd committed a violent act of revolution. They didn't press him for details. Joshua was careful to stay off the main highways to avoid the state patrol.

Marigold turned to Braden in the backseat. "Only three others at Sadie's Farm have ties to the Weather

Underground, but *nobody* in the commune has any respect for the Establishment."

"You can stay at the Farm, for two, maybe three days," Joshua said. "Then you'll have to split. The fuzz are relentless, man. It won't take 'em long to realize you didn't go to Canada, and as soon as they do, the dragnet in Washington will sweep through Oregon, maybe even California, like a tidal wave."

IV

Sadie's Farm turned out to be a smooth working enterprise. When Braden arrived, the family consisted of six women, eight men, and three small children. Difficult to determine who made up couples—if any did.

As Marigold told him when they approached the Farm, "We're not about bad vibes here. You can do your thing, as long as no one objects and it doesn't get in the way of our overall objective—to live free of restraints, but always contribute to the common good of the family."

Joshua looked Braden in the eye, "While you're here ... if you do anything to bust that vibe, you're out."

Braden was surprised to find that half the barn had been converted to art studios. Anything the artisans sold went toward supporting the commune. The rest of the barn was shared with three dairy cows and a couple of horses. The chickens and goats had pens nearby. Even though he'd only been at the Farm for twenty-four hours, Braden was impressed by the variety and quality of the vegetables and fruits produced in the huge garden. One section, covered by camouflage netting, disguised a small but hardy crop that was neither vegetable nor fruit.

The most striking feature of the place was the two-story white clapboard farmhouse. It featured several bedrooms, all of them shared, a large communal kitchen whose focal point was the wood stove, which also helped heat the house, and a long wooden trestle table where everyone ate together. Showers were a semiprivate outside event. The Farm had no television or radio. They were all comfortable operating off the grid.

While most of the members of the commune were friendly and treated him with courtesy, he was still an outsider, a fugitive who could bring the authorities down on their peaceful existence at any moment. The tension was palpable. Braden knew he'd have to take the first opportunity to move on.

He had no idea how the feds search for him was progressing, and he was desperate for news of the events at Carlyle. On the morning of his second day at the Farm, Braden volunteered to help two people who were going into Medford for supplies. He was dressed in a borrowed disguise: an old cowboy hat, sunglasses, and a well-worn peacoat.

When they stopped for herbal tea at a small café on their way out of town, Braden snagged a copy of *The Oregonian*. Once they were on the road, he buried himself in the paper. What he read felt like a shot to the gut or, more accurately, a few inches lower.

No surprise that extensive damage had been done to Carlyle's ROTC building. But his heart sank when he read that firefighters had discovered the charred body of a young woman amid the debris. The article featured his college ID photo with the caption, "Murder Suspect Braden Delaney." Fire ants raced up and down his spine, and everything went bleary. He struggled even to get a breath.

Once he could breathe more normally, Braden dove deeper into the news article. The body had been identified as Cindy Anne Parks, a freshman at Carlyle. He didn't even recognize the name. The more he read the worse the story became. Authorities claimed that the explosion was no more than a cover-up for the murder. Murder? Where the hell did they get that? Braden wasn't surprised the feds were spinning the facts to fit their own agenda but seeing the accusation in black and white froze him to the seat. The truth didn't matter to the feds; their goal was to make his bold act of revolutionary defiance something else, something much less, something much worse.

But it didn't add up. Why would this Cindy Parks have been anywhere near the ROTC building when he ignited the bomb? As far as Braden knew, no girls were part of the campus ROTC. But even if they were, damn it, he'd checked the perimeter before he broke in; he'd called out three times and looked into every room to make sure no one was there. Who would be stupid enough to run into a burning building? She must have been crazy. He *never* would have gone through with the bombing if he'd thought someone was in the building—contrary to the impression the news media was pushing.

His stomach twisted into a knot. Braden knew, in the eyes of the law, it didn't matter that he never intended to kill anyone. Intentions or not, he'd caused the explosion and fire that took a girl's life. Results were all that mattered to the FBI, not facts—especially if their suspect was already branded an anti-establishment troublemaker.

It was one thing to be part of a revolution, to stand up to the Establishment, and show the world that students were strong. A force that couldn't be bullied with guns and bayonets. But *murder*? That had never been a part of it. If Braden's act had once made him a hero of sorts among local activists, he wasn't anymore. *Murderer* was all that the name Braden Delaney would mean to anyone from now on.

This meant the manhunt would intensify for sure. The longer Braden stayed on at the Farm the more he would put the others in jeopardy. By the time they'd arrived back at Sadie's Farm, Braden's mind was made up. He had to disappear, and he had to do it fast.

Chapter 5

V

The next morning, Braden hitched a ride to Port Orford on the Oregon coast with a fellow commune member, a potter called Aurora. She told him she often delivered her work to friends in Port Orford's thriving artist community, who sold their work at summer art fairs all along the coast. More important to Braden, he'd learned the town was also a fishing port.

He didn't know how far a fishing boat traveled, but maybe he could work or buy his way onto a vessel headed somewhere south. A long shot at best, but he had to get out of the country *now*, and international waters sounded damn good at the moment. Even if he could only get a boat captain to drop him off somewhere down the coast, he'd at least have made some progress. After that, sneaking across the border into Mexico seemed like the best bet. He knew a little Spanish from school, and he figured his dark hair and complexion might help him blend in.

As it turned out, most of the fishing boats were small operations that didn't go far out to sea and returned to port with their catch each evening. No one needed an extra crewmember, especially one who had no commercial fishing experience. Braden avoided questions that might reveal his identity. He must have been pretty good at it since none of the fishermen he talked to seemed to recognize him as a notorious murderer on the run from the FBI.

By dusk, Braden had given up the fishing boat plan and hunkered down in the only café in this tiny town— drinking coffee and trying to figure out his next move. He'd been given a faded gray Stetson and a well-used denim jacket by members of the commune to help him be less conspicuous. His disguise, such as it was, seemed to be working.

He managed to find recent copies of each of the two largest newspapers in the Northwest, *The Oregonian* and the *Seattle Post-Intelligencer*. It was mortifying to see his picture still prominently displayed in every article about the case. His heart sank as he read on. The FBI was offering a thousand-dollar reward for any information leading to the capture of "suspected murderer, Braden Delaney." FBI agents were working closely with border patrols at the Canadian and Mexican borders all of whom now had Delaney's picture.

Both papers reported that because Delaney had cleaned out his bank account of several thousand dollars, authorities had intensified their presence at all the major airports in the West, as well as bus and train stations. The feds were asking anyone with immediate travel plans to keep an eye out for the fugitive but to not engage Delaney, who could be armed and dangerous.

He slumped into his chair, pulled the hat down over his brow. No one in the café showed the least bit of interest in him, but with his picture on the front pages— and he assumed, all over television—he could be spotted any second. Maybe his best move would be to head off on foot down the coast into California. Keep going until he found a boat or, better yet, a small plane that would take him out of the country. If that failed, well, California was a big state. Maybe he could lose himself in it.

He noticed a large, fifty-something man with a full dark beard sitting at a corner table. Given the guy's black fisherman's cap, Braden pegged him as a fishing boat captain or at least someone who worked on a boat. The old guy looked up from his newspaper and gave him a friendly nod. Braden didn't acknowledge it.

Tossing cash on the table, Braden made a quick exit. He checked for any police or federal agents lurking nearby, then bolted across to the doorway of an abandoned storefront and slipped into the shadows.

Almost immediately, the stranger in the black cap sauntered out of the café and did a quick reconnaissance. He crossed the street and strode past Braden's hiding place without even a glance in his direction. The guy stopped just past the doorway, leaned against the wall, and lit a cigarette. He never looked at Braden.

"Seems like me and you need to have a little talk, son," the big man said between puffs.

Braden didn't reply.

"Word on the dock is you been lookin' for a ride outta town. By the looks o' things, you ain't had much luck. And we both know you're runnin' outta time."

Braden stayed in the shadows. "I have no idea what you're talking about."

"No need to play coy, son. I seen your picture in the paper. We both know you in a boatload o' trouble." He glanced over into the shadows toward Braden. "They call me Lobo. I already know who you are." He blew out a lungful of smoke.

Braden's shoulders sagged; he was terrible at this fugitive shit. And maybe this guy *could* help. "So, what is it you want to talk to me about?"

"Well, I could be getting me a thousand bucks just for droppin' a dime on you. But, 'tween you and me, I ain't inclined to talk to feds. Besides, I got a feelin' by just doin' you a little favor I could get me more than a grand."

Braden stepped out of the shadows. "What kind of favor?"

Lobo looked him in the eye. "Let me spell it out for ya real clear, son." He raised an index finger. "One, you need a ride outta here real bad. And two," he raised a

38

second finger, "my boat, the *Swordfish*, is about to lift anchor for a trip down south."

Braden hesitated. This sounded too good to be true. "Where down south?"

Lobo let go a rusty laugh. "Come on, boy, you know it don't make no real difference where you go just so long as you can get the hell out of the States *right now*." He shot Braden a sly grin. "But since you asked, I'm headin' *way* south. Central America. That far enough away for you?"

Braden narrowed his eyes. "How do I know I can trust you?

"You don't." Lobo flipped his cigarette butt into the gutter. "But you ain't got a lot of other choices, now *do* you?"

"How the hell do I know you're not planning to sell me into slavery or something?"

Lobo looked Braden in the eye. "I don't even know how to do that. Look, it ain't my whole business, but I been known to help young guys who don't want to answer the government's call to duty. Guys who, for whatever reason, need to hide out in another country for a while."

"I'm not a draft dodger."

"Look, son, I'm just sayin' I got me plenty of experience helpin' guys your age escape the feds. All I'm doin' is trying to help another kid in need."

"Right." Braden smirked. "So, you're just a benevolent soul who's dedicated to helping draft dodgers escape the States, and you're doing this all out of the goodness of your heart."

"Mostly, yeah." Lobo shrugged. "But here's the deal son. It's simple supply and demand. You got a need, and I got a solution, but that solution ain't free."

It was time to either trust the guy or walk away. Braden sucked in a deep breath, released it. "How much?"

"Nothin' you can't afford. What say, double the reward money they're offerin'. That'd be two thousand. Cash."

Braden didn't like the sound of this. "I don't know if I can get that much."

Lobo shook his head, smirked. "No need to bullshit me, son. The papers say you emptied your bank account before leavin' town. Didn't say how much, but I'm lookin' at a fresh-scrubbed white kid who goes to an expensive private college, and I calculate you got plenty. 'Sides, I'm only wantin' a small chunk."

Braden looked Lobo up and down, thinking. *This guy's smarter than he looks ... but so am I.* "Okay, if I *can* get my hands on it. We'll do it my way—a thousand when we leave, the rest when we reach our destination."

"Fair enough." Lobo smiled, shook his head sadly. "But you gotta learn to trust people, son. I ain't greedy. Just tryin' to help a guy in need." He half-smiled. "Course, you ain't gonna be runnin' out on me on the way ... unless you're one hell of a swimmer."

"Okay, I get it." Braden still didn't completely believe Lobo's claim of helping young guys escape the draft. He suspected the purpose of the boat's journey to Central America was much less benevolent than that. Didn't matter at this point. He quickly ran through his other options. He could try to travel the length of California on foot, hoping no one would recognize him. He could hide out somewhere knowing at any moment the feds could rush in and nab him. Or he could turn himself in, explain things and let them throw the book at him, leaving him to rot in prison until they got around to sending him to the gas chamber.

Braden eased out a breath. "How soon?"

"You in luck, son. Tonight. I like to make my departures after dark. Less hassle that way." He grinned. "Also, a lot easier to sneak a passenger aboard." He checked the darkening sky. "We got us a nice marine layer comin' in. Fog's already building. You show up down by the pier, say, in an hour ... *with* the thousand bucks, and we might could do some business. If you're late, the deal's off. Me and the *Swordfish* will be long gone, and you'll be stuck in this burg, lookin' over your shoulder, waitin' for the FBI to nab you. Hell, for all we know some upstanding local citizen coulda already made the call to the feds." With that, he strolled off down the sidewalk.

Braden watched him disappear into the night. Whatever he'd face aboard the *Swordfish*, it was still his best option.

My lower back was stiff. That's why they tell you to get up from your desk every fifteen minutes or so. I stretched as I walked over to the window and looked down at the street below. Hardly a surprise that people were going through their day as if nothing had changed. I knew every one of them. And every one of them knew Dad.

I pictured Dad stopping to talk with whoever wanted to chew the fat. The chill that rushed through my body caught me by surprise. But this wasn't the time to be staring out the window reminiscing. I spun around, headed back to my desk and my appointment with Braden Delaney.

Chapter 6

VI

Braden's voyage on the *Swordfish* didn't turn out to be as dangerous as he feared, but it quickly became tedious and boring. He didn't realize that a boat moving in open water felt like it was going a hell of a lot slower than it was. And he hadn't expected it to be so damn windy and cold aboard ship, even when the sun was high above. Most of all, he didn't anticipate spending most of the first couple of days puking his guts out over the side.

Braden stayed mostly to himself inside the cabin next to the *Swordfish*'s small galley. Lobo and his three-man crew treated Braden more like an inconvenient guest than a fugitive. No one besides Lobo paid much attention to him, except to scrunch over to make a place for him during meals. The crew spoke Spanish exclusively. What

Braden had been taught in high school and during his two years at Carlyle had been formal Castilian Spanish. None of the crew were speaking Castilian. He wasn't sure it was even Spanish. He laughed when they laughed and nodded agreement when it felt appropriate. He just didn't always know what he was laughing about or agreeing with.

He overheard enough to understand that, although the *Swordfish's* hold was empty now, on the trip back from *Centroamérica* the boat would be loaded with something only referred to as *la captura*, the catch. Braden guessed either marijuana or cocaine.

They'd been at sea almost a week when the *Swordfish* slowed and Lobo cut the engine. Must have finally reached its destination, which according to what Braden had overheard was somewhere in Nicaragua. Fine with him. The moment they arrived in port, he would pay Lobo the second thousand, disappear into the local scenery, and then … well, then he'd figure out what to do next.

Surely, he'd be able to get by wherever he ended up. He was smart and resourceful, and he'd have plenty

45

of cash to convert to pesos or whatever the local currency might be. In his experience, money had always smoothed the way. With luck, no one would even pay any attention to a stranger with the American accent. If this were to be his new life, he would make the most of it. But despite his self-assurances, he'd never felt more alone or more anxious.

Braden stepped out on the deck and took in the view. It was dusk, not so dark that he wouldn't be able to make out land. He saw nothing but ocean in every direction. His muscles tightened, and he hid his trembling hands in the pockets of his jeans. What the hell was going on?

He caught Lobo's eye. "Why stop clear out here? Are we even close to land?"

Lobo smirked. "We're 'bout three miles offshore is all. Waitin' for the sun to drop all the way down before we head into port. We work best in the dark."

"Thanks for helping me out, man." Braden managed a half smile.

Lobo shrugged. "We had a deal. I've done my part. Now it's time to do yours. Just like we agreed."

Braden glanced at the open water, then affected his best serious look. "I'll hand over the other thousand as soon as I'm on land."

Lobo shook his head. "Nope, gonna have to be now. We get pretty busy loading our cargo once we reach shore. We need to get in and out as fast as possible. Ain't gonna have time to be exchangin' cash … especially with so many witnesses around."

"I'm not—"

"Trust me, you wouldn't make it ten feet before you were robbed and left for dead." He sneered. "And we both know you gotta keep a low profile. So, once we make the beach, you best sneak away real quick like."

Braden cringed.

Lobo placed his hand gently on Braden's shoulder. "Only thinkin' of your safety, son."

"I appreciate that," Braden said, despite the tightness in his chest. He wasn't buying this kindly parent act.

Lobo tilted his head to the side and held out an open palm.

Braden got the point. "Right. Just give me a sec." He slipped deeper into the ship's cabin, stepped into the head, and closed the door. In the dim light from the single bare bulb overhead, he opened his jacket, lifted his shirt, and pulled away the plastic bag taped to his stomach. He counted out a thousand dollars, slipped the bills into the pocket of his jeans. Then he rewrapped the bag, taped it shut, and shoved it to the bottom of his backpack.

Back on deck, he handed Lobo the money.

Without even looking at it, Lobo slipped the wad of cash inside his pea coat. "Good doin' business with you, son." He offered his hand.

Braden shook it like a man.

Lobo rolled his eyes, then snapped his fingers. "Jesus. Almost forgot." He shook his head. "Gettin' too old I guess." He nodded to Braden. "You and me gotta do one more thing before we head in."

Braden felt a burning fist in his stomach. He scrunched up his face.

Lobo grinned. "Relax, kid. I'm only askin' that you'd do this ol' sea dog the courtesy of joinin' me."

Braden raised an eyebrow. "Joining you?"

48

"Yep. See, there's this long-standin' tradition for when a sea captain completes a successful voyage." His gaze drifted out to the ocean. "Kind of like payin' honor to the sea gods for bein' granted safe passage. Called Neptune's Salute."

Braden supposed that could be a legitimate thing. Even so, he felt the color draining from his cheeks, his muscles tightening.

Lobo let out a hearty laugh. "Don't worry, son. Ain't nothin' but a fancy excuse for drinkin' a toast."

Braden let out a pent-up breath. "Well, then I'd be happy to join you in the salute."

Lobo looked around, turned back to Braden, and whispered, "You keep a watch on the crew while I slip inside. Don't have much of the good stuff left. Not enough to share with this lot."

Braden checked out the two crew members smoking portside. "Oh, right. Got it."

Lobo winked and disappeared inside the cabin.

After nearly five minutes, Braden started to wonder what was taking Lobo so long. He was about to step inside to find out when the big man reappeared holding two tin coffee cups: each appeared to be half full of a dark gold liquid.

Lobo handed one to Braden. "Sorry about takin' so long, but this is from my own special bottle of rum, and I forgot where I hid the damn thing. Memory ain't what it used to be." He held up his cup. "To Neptune."

Braden followed suit. Then looked into the cup, sniffed it. Jesus, it smelled like straight rum.

Lobo nodded to him. "Best to drink it like a sailor, boy. It's a toast. You gotta throw it down all at once. Like this." He tipped his cup and emptied the whole thing down his throat. Blew out a loud sigh and shook his head a couple of times as if to clear it.

Braden rarely drank hard liquor, but whenever he had, he'd sipped it. Not an option this time. He took in a breath, let it out, and downed his drink. The rum burned all the way down to his gut where it landed with a thump.

Lobo reached over and took the cup from him. "I'd offer you more, son. But like I said, this is rare stuff. I only bring it out for ceremonies and such."

Braden nodded his understanding. He wasn't anxious to repeat this particular ceremony anyway.

Lobo looked out at the water. "It's almost black dark. Time to get a move on." He handed the cups to Braden. "Drop these in the galley sink, and make sure you got everything packed up, boy." He gave Braden a fatherly pat on the shoulder. "We'll be puttin' you ashore right soon."

With that, he turned and spat out a series of rapid-fire instructions, which sent the crew into a flurry of activity. Almost immediately the boat surged into the night, with no running lights.

Braden felt a little woozy. He hoped it wasn't a sign his seasickness was back now that the boat was underway again. He didn't want his first act in a foreign country to be throwing up all over the beach. He sat down on the deck to steady himself against the motion of the sea.

Then, he slowly drifted into blackness.

Chapter 7

VII

Braden eased his eyes open barely a slit, but even that much was painful. The sun scalded him like a blast furnace. His head throbbed. His throat was so parched he could barely swallow—and it hurt like hell when he tried. Where *was* he? He tried to sit upright, but it made him so woozy he leaned back against the side. The side? He turned his head slightly to the left, winced in pain. Looked like he was floating in a small wooden skiff, but he couldn't tell if the current was taking him toward land or farther out to sea. How the hell did he get *here*?

The last thing Braden remembered was drinking a toast to Neptune. Now, the sun was almost directly overhead. That meant there were twelve hours or so he couldn't account for. Even though he wasn't used to drinking straight rum, he'd downed less than half a cup. That shouldn't have been enough to make him black out. Unless Lobo… shit!

His heart was pounding fast, too fast. He choked trying to take in a breath. Willing himself to calm down, he managed to get his breathing back toward normal. He scanned the skiff for his backpack. Gone. Damn it. No pack meant no clothes, no supplies, no money. The bastards had even taken his shoes and socks. He'd never felt so stupid … or so naive. Tough lesson learned.

The oars were missing. Figures. That meant he had one option—paddle with his hands to safety. He was probably close to Nicaragua since that's where the *Swordfish* was allegedly headed. If only he could figure out which direction would lead him there. He pushed himself up onto an elbow, twisted around,. and squinted against the glare off the water, trying to catch sight of land. Couldn't make out anything. Even that little movement made him light-headed; he was about to pass out. Everything hurt. He'd never had a migraine, but it couldn't be any worse than the way his head felt at the moment. Yes, he was still alive. At least Lobo hadn't just thrown him overboard after he blacked out. But he might as well be stranded in the middle of the ocean. Maybe he was.

He had so much trouble trying to control his limbs, it took him three tries to grab the side of the boat and pull himself up. Then his head started spinning, and he had to wait for the dizziness to subside. As soon as he leaned over the side to paddle with his hands, a wave of nausea smacked him like a sucker punch. He tumbled backward and slid back into darkness.

VIII

When he came to this time, he remembered he was in a small boat—with nothing but his T-shirt and jeans to his name—but he seemed to be moving more deliberately than before. He must have caught some sort of current. He opened one eye and immediately squeezed it shut. The sun remained his brutal enemy. Braden forced himself up as best he could to try to get his bearings. Shading his eyes with his free hand, he was able to make out a large shadowy shape floating in front of his skiff. A huge dolphin? A whale? Whatever it was, he seemed to be following it. When the hell was he going to wake up from this dream, this nightmare?

But as the shape slowly came into focus, Braden saw he was being towed by another boat, occupied by a man, dressed in white and wearing a frazzled sombrero.

He offered Braden a broad smile. "*Buenas tardes, señor.*"

Braden tried to answer. "*Buenas t...*" was as far as he got.

The man pulled Braden's boat alongside and handed him a gourd. The first sip of water felt like a cool mountain stream against Braden's chapped and bleeding lips. He took a healthier swallow. Then he threw it up.

"*Bebe a sorbos,*" the man said with a grin.

Braden tried to shake his head to show he didn't understand, but it hurt too much.

The man took back the gourd, raised it to his lips, and took a small sip before he handed it back.

This time Braden sipped a little at a time until he'd had enough. "*Gracias,*" he rasped, as he handed back the gourd. He had lots of questions, but too little Spanish and not enough mental capacity at the moment to ask them.

He wasn't confident he could even control his arms and legs much less speak properly. What the hell had Lobo slipped him in that drink?

The guy motioned downward with his hands. "*Usted debe descansar.*"

Braden wasn't sure about the words, but he understood the gesture. He eased himself back down, closed his eyes, and waited for the blackness to engulf him.

◆ ◆ ◆

The skiff scraping the shore jarred him awake. Land! He opened his eyes just enough to see five or six shacks huddled together like a pathetic legion poised to fend off invaders. He heard several voices, all murmuring in Spanish. Four men carried Braden on a makeshift stretcher into a crude shelter and laid him down on a cot.

Everyone left but the man who'd rescued him and a young girl, who looked to be about sixteen. She was wearing a faded red headscarf and a not-quite-matching dress that hung on her slight frame and scraped along the ground. The two of them exchanged a few urgent words in Spanish, and she hurried out.

The girl returned with a bowl of soapy water, some clean rags, and a narrow gourd. She helped Braden sit up, handed him the gourd, and steadied his hands so he could drink. Too weak to protest, he sipped the pungent, bitter concoction. It wasn't easy to get down, but he sensed it was meant to help him with his nausea, even ease his pain. Wishful thinking maybe. At least he didn't throw it up.

The girl faced Braden's rescuer, whispered, *"¿Quién este?"*

Braden understood she was asking who he was.

The man shrugged, *"No lo sé. ¿Tal vez él es de los Estados Unidos?"*

The girl turned to Braden, *"Mi hermano,* Filipe, think you *es* from United Estates? *¿Es verdad?"*

Braden managed to whisper, *"Sí."* Grateful she seemed to know a little English.

That's when a rotund older woman, in a colorful head scarf and shawl over her long, bright blue dress burst into the room. *"¡Dios mio! ¡Es Diego! Él ha vuelto a nosotros."* She knelt and enveloped Braden, hugging him tighter than he expected she could. Strands of salt-and-pepper hair escaped from her headscarf.

"*¡No, mamá!*" The girl took her mother by the shoulders, eased her upright. "*Él no es Diego. Él es un extranjero … de Norteamérica.*"

The woman shook her head vigorously, never taking her eyes off Braden. "*No-no-no, es Diego.*" She clasped Braden's hand in hers, tilted her head to the sky. "*Gracias a Dios.*" Filipe gently took her by the arm and led her out the door.

The girl sighed and turned to Braden. "*Mi mamá*, she believe you her *hijo*, Diego, who *es* lost at sea *dos años* … two year. She still weep for him all the nights. I tried say her you no Diego … *pero* she no listen."

Braden patted her arm. "It's okay, *entiendo*."

She looked him over. "*¿Qual es tu nombre?*"

She wanted his name. Tricky. "*Realmente … mi nombre es Diego.*" He managed a crooked smile.

She rolled her eyes. "*Bien … si tu lo dices.*"

Braden cringed; she wasn't buying it.

She gestured to herself. "*Yo soy Juanita … Juanita Molina.*"

Braden, feeling drowsy, managed a nod and a question. *"¿Dónde estoy?"*

She gestured toward the door of the hut. *"Este es El Salvador."* You esleep now. I carry to you food after." With that, she left.

IX

By the next day, Braden's condition had improved. He still had no recollection of what had happened to him aboard the Swordfish after he downed the rum—and whatever was in it—but he felt the headache subsiding and nausea was no longer his constant companion. Whatever liquid Juanita was giving him seemed to help. Maybe in a day or two, he'd regain most of his strength and stamina.

Given the smells and activity outside the hut, Braden surmised he'd been brought to a small fishing village on the Salvadoran coast.

By now, Señora Molina had told everyone in the tiny village about the miracle of her son Diego's return from the sea. The old woman had checked on Braden several times since he arrived, often accompanied by curiosity seekers from the village, and entertaining them with nonstop animated babbling in Spanish. He picked up enough to guess she wasn't letting go of her fantasy.

Through Juanita, Filipe warned Braden that word of his arrival—and the miracle return of their brother, Diego—was quickly spreading to nearby villages. He assumed Braden was *un fugitivo.* Juanita told him that Filipe didn't care who he was running from. But her brother feared the family would have to pay a stiff price when word of the stranger's arrival reached either *la policía* or *la milicia,* who were always harsh and usually cruel.

Braden got it. Complete recovery or not, it was time for him to go.

Juanita cautioned him that it would be safer for him to leave after dark. And as soon as the sun dipped into the ocean, she returned carrying food and a large gourd of water wrapped in a cloth bundle, along with a clean white shirt, a poncho, a slightly torn straw cowboy hat, and a pair of sandals.

Figuring Braden would want to keep out of sight as much as possible, she told him he should head for

Honduras—Nicaragua wasn't a good option, too much violence—but she warned him it would be dangerous to claim to be Salvadoran once he reached Honduras. Tension still ran high after *La Guerra Del Fútbol*, the Soccer War, between Honduras and El Salvador just last year.

Juanita drew him a crude map of the inland route to *el Río Lempa*, where he might be able to find *un barco* to take him north into Honduras. A trek of close to fifty kilometers, but if he stuck close to the main roads, there was a chance someone might give him a ride part of the way. The long trek would be worth it, though, because once he reached the river, he'd have a quicker route into the mountains across the Honduran border.

It was clear to Braden that, if he hoped to survive in Central America, he had a hell of a lot to learn in a short time—and not just the language. He thanked her in Spanish, hugged her goodbye, and set out into the night.

"*Buena suerte ... Diego*," she called after him.

Braden waved back just before the darkness swallowed him whole.

I worked my sore neck back and forth, stepped away from the manuscript. Felt like I was getting a headache. Did that mean I was channeling Braden Delaney? No, my angry stomach let me know I just needed to eat something. I stepped into my kitchenette. Grilled cheese sounded good, smelled better. I devoured it.

I set my plate in the sink and grabbed a Corona from the refrigerator. Since the narrative was now in Central America, it seemed only appropriate to break open a cerveza.

Chapter 8

X

Braden's progress toward the Lempa River was plodding from the first. Physically he still hadn't gotten his full strength back; his arms and legs still didn't always work the way he expected. But he had enough perseverance to keep moving forward. His motivation was to put as much distance between him and whoever might be tracking him—if not the feds, then possibly the Salvadoran militia would be on his trail once they got wind of Señora Molina's miracle. Hell, maybe no one was chasing him. Nonetheless, he couldn't help constantly looking over his shoulder, knowing that at any moment he could be attacked, robbed, even killed simply because he was a stranger.

Even though his feet were soon blistered and his legs ached, he tramped as far as he could each day, resting only a few minutes at a time. He did his best to be back on the road before sunup. The afternoon sun was not his friend, but he suffered the heat as long he could each day until he had to take refuge for a few minutes in a shady spot when he could find one. He lost his sense of direction easily, so he regularly traced his progress on Juanita's map, which indicated he was still inching his way toward the Lempa. But after several days on the road, the river felt farther away than when he started.

Braden ate little each day, rationing his provisions to try to make them last until he could figure out a way to get food. Juanita had packed several flatbread-like things she called *pupusas*, thick as pancakes and stuffed with cheese, refried beans, and fish. A little spicy, but delicious. He could only afford to eat half of one at a time if he hoped to make them last. She'd also included slices of dried fish, which he tore into small pieces to make them easier to gnaw on while walking.

He managed to find sources to replenish his water gourd in some of the small villages he passed through.

The local water supply often proved to be less than sanitary, and that meant more than a few emergency stops along the way. But after a week his system adjusted. Despite his efforts to preserve his food supply, though, soon it was as exhausted as he was.

At night, he bedded down wherever he could find a secluded area off the road, using the poncho as a blanket. He slept in short spurts. Who knew who might be lurking in the dark waiting for an opportunity to rob him, or worse. And there was still a chance he had the Salvadoran military on his trail.

He was more alone, more desperate than he'd ever been in his life. He'd been thrust into the middle of a foreign country, and he barely knew the language. His only possessions were the clothes he wore. He had no money, and no way to earn any. He faced a future always on the run, always a stranger. For his own safety, he had to avoid contact with people—at least until he managed to get farther inland. If he even made it that far.

He'd escaped the authorities, for the time being anyway, but he'd never see his own country again. And worst of all, he'd lost Cheryl Stevens, the love of his life. Forever.

XI

Several days later, he didn't know how many exactly. He'd lost track of the days of the week long ago. Braden couldn't take another step; he slumped to the ground at the side of the dirt road. He'd done it before, but this time it felt like the end. "Despair" wasn't a big enough word to cover it. He hadn't eaten in three days, his legs ached constantly, and his feet were bleeding and blistered. Was this how it was all going to end?

He glanced back down the road at the sound of a vehicle heading his way. His muscles froze, and a sharp pain slashed through his stomach. Didn't look like the authorities, though. The ancient pickup came to a stop. It may once have been blue, but now it looked to be mostly rust, with splotches of washed-out color.

An old man and a lanky teenager climbed down from the truck and approached Braden. *"¿Esta bien?"* the man asked.

Braden slowly raised his head, his eyes blank.

The kid crouched down. *"¿Necesita ayuda?* You need help?"

Braden managed a nod and a weak smile. Thank God. The boy must have studied some English in school.

The old man gestured to the boy. *"Este es mi nieto, Julio."* He patted his chest. *"Yo soy Santos."* He held out a gnarled hand.

Braden shook it. *"Yo soy Diego."*

In a conversation laced with broken Spanish and broken English, Diego told them he was headed for *El Río Lempa.* Julio, who it turned out was Santos' grandson, helped Diego understand that they were hauling used tractor parts to be transported upstream to hand over to a cousin, Alfredo, who would haul them to his farm several kilometers inside the Honduran border. Even though Diego protested, they shared their meager food with him. Cold tortillas and beans had never tasted so heavenly

Given Diego's fumbling attempts to converse in Spanish, his companions quickly guessed he was *inglés,* not Salvadoran. He acknowledged his *Norteaméricano* roots, but he didn't offer any specifics. When Santos suggested Diego ride with them the rest of the way to *El*

Rio Lempa, he accepted. It was his destination, after all; besides he didn't have the energy to argue.

They reached the river at dusk, and Diego helped load the tractor parts onto a small barge, then joined the others on board for the trip north.

The trip up the Lempa took nearly three days. The other passengers included an old milk cow and eight constantly protesting goats. The other humans aboard, besides Santos, Julio, and Diego, were a couple of surly farmers, who watched over the animals, and Emerson, the boat pilot. The farmers took the animals ashore early the second day. Diego's sense of relief was palpable. He'd never experienced either never-ending clamor or gag-inducing smell of animals at close quarters. The only time he'd been this close to farm animals was when his kindergarten class took a field trip to a petting zoo.

The three days on the river with little to do gave Diego a chance to practice his language skills with Julio and Emerson. By the time they unloaded the tractor parts onto a rickety dock well inside Honduras, Braden had recalled some of the Spanish he'd studied in school and added several new words to his Spanish vocabulary. Most local idioms, though, still escaped him. No one was going to mistake him for a native speaker any time soon. He was well aware that if word got out that a pale, non-native speaker had been in the area, the U.S. authorities might well follow up. He hoped to be long gone into the interior of Honduras before they had a chance.

The cousin was not at the dock to meet them as planned. With no way to communicate with Alfredo, Santos and his grandson were concerned they might be stuck waiting for days. They were needed back at their farm for the early corn harvest. The boat had other stops to make further upstream, but Emerson promised to pick up Santos and Julio on the return trip the next afternoon. They moved the tractor parts from the dock and made a crude camp nearby, where they spent an uneasy night, partly because Santos regaled them with accounts of violence against Salvadorans by Hondurans.

When Alfredo still hadn't arrived by the time the boat returned the next afternoon, Diego volunteered to stay and guard the tractor parts until the cousin arrived. He considered it small compensation for sharing their food and for their kindness. Santos and Julio were visibly relieved and only too happy to accept Diego's offer. Through Julio, the old man assured Diego that Alfredo could be relied upon and that he would show up as promised … eventually.

It wasn't until the following evening that Alfredo Alcázar finally showed up at the dock. Braden introduced himself as Diego Molina. As soon as he said the name, he realized that alias could be a huge mistake if the Salvadoran authorities were after him. That was the name Mamá Molina would have mentioned when she related the miracle of her son's return from the sea … and his disappearance from the village. Too late now. He needed to be more careful, smarter. Another lesson learned.

He didn't catch all the details of Alcázar's explanation for his tardiness, but it seemed to have something to do with a borrowed truck and the long trip from his farm several hours away. He and Diego loaded the parts into the truck bed and tied them down tight. Important, as Alfredo explained, because of the poor condition of some of the roads.

Alfredo told Diego he was bringing the tractor parts to the small subsistence farm his family owned in

Honduras. After a few starts and stops, Diego managed to communicate that he hoped to find *un trabajo*, a job. Alcázar looked him over, shrugged, and said, *"¿Por qué no?"* Then he headed for the truck.

Maybe it was the Honduran pronunciation or an idiom Diego didn't know, but it seemed like Alcázar didn't care whether Diego needed work or not. Alcázar twisted back around when he realized Diego hadn't moved. He waved his hand toward the passenger seat. Diego may still have been confused by the language, but he was getting pretty good at reading gestures.

Chapter 9

On the trip to the farm, Alberto explained to Diego that, the family patriarch, Humberto Alcázar, was getting on in years and wasn't able to put in long hours in the fields or even take care of the essential chores anymore. Diego could take some of the burden off the old man's shoulders.

The Alcázars' farm was small, less than twenty acres including the pasture. Aside from seasonal fruit, they grew mostly corn, beans, and enough sorghum to feed the livestock. Two cows and three nanny goats were sources of milk and butter, and a couple of horses helped with the plowing and provided transportation. They produced enough surplus to trade for coffee, sugar, and other necessities.

The current iteration of the family consisted of Humberto, Alfredo, his pregnant wife, Gabriella, and their two small children, Xander, seven years old, and Larissa, five. That meant the small, well-kept farmhouse was full. But there was always room for Diego at the table for meals, and he had no qualms about sleeping in the barn. Drafty, but the Alcázars provided plenty of blankets, and after a while, Diego got used to the animal stench.

Under the old man's supervision, Diego quickly mastered the mundane but essential tasks, including cleaning the stables and feeding and milking the cows and goats. Xander and Larissa taught him how to feed the chickens.

Humberto told Diego he'd brought his family to Honduras years ago to escape Franco's tyrannical dictatorship in Spain. The old man proudly pointed out that Alcázar was an old, respected Spanish name, not traditional Honduran.

In less than a month, Diego was working alongside Alfredo, clearing land, digging irrigation ditches, and helping plant crops. Once they'd upgraded the old tractor with the parts they'd brought back with them from the *Río*

Lempa, plowing and other chores were much easier. Diego received no pay, and he worked hard for his keep. Fine with him, he was grateful for the Alcázars hospitality and kindness.

The farm rarely had visitors, which suited Diego just fine. He made sure he stayed out of sight whenever someone stopped by. Gabriella was anxious to introduce him to her niece, Consuela, reported to be a real beauty. He didn't doubt that Consuela was as lovely as her aunt described, but it hadn't yet been a year since Braden had left behind his one true love. Cheryl Stevens was still very much on his mind and in his heart.

XIII

After six months on the Alcázars' farm, Diego was getting restless. Staying very long in one place made him too vulnerable. He had no way of knowing if the authorities were still on his trail. By now he was much better able to get by on his own. His command of Honduran Spanish had grown considerably, and the physically taxing farm work made him healthier and stronger than he'd ever been.

When he told the Alcázars he was planning to move on, they protested, especially the children. In just six months, he'd become part of the family. But Alfredo understood a young man's need to be independent, and he relayed a rumor that the seasonal workers on a large farm nearby would soon be heading off to the next job— working the coffee harvest on a plantation some twenty kilometers to the east. Diego jumped at the opportunity to join *los trabajadores migratorios*. Even if he couldn't find work in the coffee fields, moving farther inland would make it more difficult for the authorities to track him down.

Soon it was time for him to go, and the family gathered in the small yard next to the house. Diego said his sad goodbyes, the children clinging to his legs begging him not to leave. Gabriella hugged him, then pressed a leather bag full of food, clothing, and supplies into his arms. She spun around and walked back to the house, the children at her side, before Diego had a chance to protest her kind gesture. He wiped away a tear and shook hands with Alfredo and Humberto one last time, then he set off on foot for the farm a few kilometers down the road.

XIV

Since he was a stranger, the migrants were suspicious of Diego at first, but they were willing to include him in their group, mostly because they knew there would be plenty of work for everyone in a coffee bean harvest. This newcomer wouldn't be taking jobs away from any of them. On the long bus ride to the plantation, he joined in conversations as best he could. But he mostly kept to himself.

As predicted, the plantation manager hired the entire group. He signed on as "Diego Alcázar." He figured old Humberto would be okay with it, maybe even proud. And it might be more difficult to pick up his trail. At this point, though, he hoped the Salvadoran authorities had just lost interest in him. If they'd ever had any. He figured the attention span of U.S. pursuers would be longer.

Diego was hired as a coffee picker, one of the lowest-ranking jobs on the plantation. The irony of his situation wasn't lost on him. Most often, immigrants to the United States who spoke English poorly had to settle for the menial jobs and low pay—even if they had an adequate education or the skills for something much better. Here in Honduras, Diego found himself at the bottom of the migrant pecking order. The lowest of the low. He spent long, exhausting days in the hot sun, and occasionally in driving rain, for forty Honduran Lempira per day—less than two dollars American. Disheartening for sure, but given his privileged upbringing, it felt like a kind of cosmic justice to him.

Soon enough, Diego began to fit in with the other workers, but he stayed mostly on the periphery. The male workers all slept together in rundown, drafty wooden shacks. The crude cots were so crowded together it was difficult to move around at night. No pillows or blankets were provided. Privacy was nonexistent. But soon enough he adapted to the harsh conditions. He earned some measure of respect from the other migrants because he worked hard without complaint. And it was noticed by the overseers. He was kept on for the whole season.

He had no access to U.S. newspapers, and local news didn't bother with the plight of an American college student who might be on the FBI's Most Wanted List. Likely no one back home knew he'd escaped on the *Swordfish*. After all, that bastard Lobo wouldn't be offering any details. Even so, he found himself constantly looking over his shoulder, suspicious of anyone he didn't immediately recognize. He wasn't confident he could even trust all his fellow migrants.

Left alone with his thoughts, Braden still suffered painful bouts of remorse. Not so much for blowing up the ROTC building, but for poor Cindy Anne Parks who'd been trapped inside. The feds wouldn't care that he never meant to harm anyone—they wanted him for murder.

When work on the coffee plantation ended, Diego boarded a beat-up bus with most of the migrant crew and headed north. His pack now contained fresh clothes, a few personal belongings—all purchased at exorbitant prices at the company store—and a small cache of hard-earned *lempiras*. Following the crops, lost in a crowd of *migratorios*, felt like a damn good cover.

The ringing of my cell brought me out of my reverie. Mom. Checking on me.

"Just wanted to see how you were doing, honey. Feeling any better?"

What was she talking about? Wait. Oh, right. I'm supposed to be sick. "A little better. I think I just needed some sleep." My head was a little fuzzy since my brain had just made an instant transition from Honduras in the Seventies to Shoat Valley in 2012.

"Sorry to wake you, Nick. But Corinne Aster called about Ann Patchett's newest, *State of Wonder*. She said she ordered it two days ago. I was hoping you might know its status."

"Let me think."

"I wouldn't bother you, but she seems anxious. You know how she can be when she's upset."

"Oh yeah. I know. That's why I checked this morning. Figured she'd pester us about it. Tell her it's supposed to be delivered by end of day tomorrow."

"Thanks, I'll let her know. Now you get back to sleep. Let me know if you need anything later."

I will. Bye, Mom." I shook myself, took in a deep breath to clear my head of the present-time reality, and dove back into the manuscript.

Chapter 10

XV

Diego worked his way across Honduras over the next five years, joining various migrant groups as they traveled from one harvest to the next. But he never stayed in one plantation or with the same group for more than a season. He picked bananas and coffee beans and chopped sugar cane, work that was always exhausting, but he was thankful for anything he could get.

In time, Diego became immersed in the language well enough that he contributed to conversations and even loosened up a little when he and his companions let off steam in the evenings. He managed to fit in with each of the groups he joined. For the most part, though, he stayed to himself. While his relations with others were friendly, they were never close.

Diego had more than his share of opportunities for intimate relationships with migrant women in the camps. He did his best to avoid sexual encounters. Morals were loose, but sex among *los migratorios* in the camps had a dark side. He witnessed the brutal retribution from jealous boyfriends or protective relatives foisted on men who had crossed the line. Diego turned a blind eye to these attacks. He didn't fully understand the cultural issues behind the violence, but he did know it wasn't his place to intervene. On some plantations, women lived in constant fear of being raped and beaten by other *trabajadores* or, more often, by *supervisores*, overseers hired by the owners to keep the migrants in line.

Even though some of the women were tenacious in their pursuit of Diego, he refused to reciprocate. He was still true to Cheryl. Yes, by now she'd probably found a new love, but cheating on her still felt wrong to Diego. After a few years though, despite his resoluton, he began to give in to the passion of the moment. In the end, a young man has itches that have to be scratched. Still, he was careful to avoid more serious relationships, much to the chagrin of a few of the women.

In the fall of 1974, news reached the migrant camps of Hurricane Fifi slamming the Caribbean coast of Honduras, killing as many as ten thousand and leaving thousands more homeless. Since Diego stayed mostly in the mountain regions, he was safe enough from the devastation of the hurricane, but the storm destroyed the country's entire banana crop. No harvest meant no work.

With jobs scarce and tempers short, the competition among *los migratorios* for the few jobs still available was intense. Fights broke out, most often the result of too much local beer, or when they could get it, *guaro,* a kind of moonshine made from sugar cane.

As much as he tried to keep a low profile, Diego couldn't escape the inevitable shouting match, fistfight, or worse. Still an outsider, he was an easy target. Over time, he'd learned the importance of maintaining machismo. He never started a skirmish, but when confronted and forced to save face, he stood up to the taunting and defended his honor like a man. He gave as good as he got, but more than once he suffered painful scrapes and bruises or had to be treated for knife wounds.

His most serious wound came when he jumped into the fray to help out Andres Hernandez, the closest thing Diego had to a friend. Andres was attacked by two other migrants, both wielding knives. When Diego came upon the scene, one of the thugs was holding Andres while the other one drove a curved nine-inch banana knife into Andres's stomach and twisted it. Diego plowed into the one holding Andres and all four tumbled to the ground. He fought with both culprits, dodging the blades and delivering debilitating blows and kicks to the attackers.

When the *supervisores* finally arrived, the knife-wielders ran off, leaving Diego to tend to Andres. But it was too late for his friend. Diego had no time to mourn. He'd been slashed in the lower back during the scuffle and his clothes were covered in blood. They carried Diego to the crude onsite infirmary, where he was stitched up, given a few pain pills, and sent back to the barracks to recover as best he could. As much treatment as he expected. He learned that Andres's body had simply been dumped in a pit like so much roadkill. *That* he hadn't expected.

XVI

By now, Diego has acquired legal-looking Honduran identification papers, complete with his photo — he now had longer hair, a dark tan, and a full beard. All it took was sufficient lempira and someone with connections who didn't ask questions. Because he was now proficient in Honduran Spanish, most people he encountered assumed he was *Honureño,* a local term for a Honduran. When he stumbled over a phrase or pronunciation, he might be asked what country he grew up in, but no one suspected he was American.

Diego became more and more acclimated to the lifestyle and the questionable morality of the Honduran migrant culture. But beneath his façade lurked a stranger pretending to fit in. Though he spent his time with others in the field and in the crowded workers' quarters, he still led a lonely life. A life worlds away from the future he'd once imagined.

He often thought of writing Cheryl and his family, just to let someone know he was alive. He missed them. He missed home. He composed a letter to his father and mother, apologizing for his rash actions and seeking forgiveness, but he destroyed it before he had a chance to mail it. He didn't know how his father and mother felt about what he had done—even if the murder *was* an accident. But a letter postmarked in Honduras would be a red flag to the FBI. As far as he knew, they were still after him. Same reason he never wrote to Cheryl. With the authorities monitoring her for sure, it was just too dangerous to remind the feds of her association with Braden Delaney.

But he had another good reason for not writing to Cheryl. By this point, he'd been gone for nearly seven years. She was probably married with a couple of kids by now. She would have moved far away from Sinclair, so he didn't know how to reach her anyway. Most of all, though, he didn't want to interfere with whatever new life she'd made for herself. In the end, he decided that it would be best if everyone back home considered Braden Delaney dead. Like he did.

◆ ◆ ◆

I rubbed my eyes. Good place to take a break. I grabbed another beer.

85

Sixteen segments in, the ink color had switched from blue to black and back again. I pictured Dad sneaking off to write another section whenever he got the chance.

It would have been hard for Dad to portray the life of a loner in a foreign land. He was always so focused on family and community. He attended every game, every play, every event that Shelby or I were involved in. We loved having him there cheering us on. We counted on it.

Mom and Dad were in the audience when I graduated from Sonoma State. Shelby was finishing her junior year at UC Santa Barbara.

Dad wouldn't be attending her graduation.

Chapter 11

XVII

In the spring of 1977, Diego heard that the Sandinista rebels—across the southern border in Nicaragua— were desperate to reinforce their revolutionary army. The migrants lived in fear that the rebels would escalate their already brazen "recruiting" of entire crews of Honduran field workers, forcing them to join the fight against the Somoza dictatorship.

Reports reached Diego's group that anyone who refused suffered brutal torture before they were killed. Women had it worse. They were physically and sexually abused even if they agreed to join forces with the Sandinistas. Word was, none of the kidnapped *migratorios* was ever heard from again.

In the middle of the night, Diego was awakened by frantic screams from the women's quarters. He rushed to the door and eased it open enough to see a ragtag group of soldiers dragging some of the women outside, while others ran for their lives toward the dense forest that surrounded the plantation. The captured women fought viciously, but they were no match for the two or three soldiers who held them down. Diego knew these rebels would round up every man in the camp and thrust them into the thick of the fighting in Nicaragua. He saw immediately there was no way they could reach the cache of banana knives in the fields. Besides these rebels had guns, and they clearly weren't afraid to use them. There was nothing the male workers could do to save the women.

The men's barracks became a frenzy of pushing, shoving, and clawing at the single door. Each man who rushed out was run down and captured. Those who made it too far to grab were simply gunned down.

Diego grabbed the few possessions he had, broke out the back window of the barracks, and ran for his life into the dark forest. Others followed suit, but only Diego and a few others outran the rebels. Once they'd escaped, they separated for their own safety and struck out into the thick of the rainforest.

Four days later Diego made it to a remote railroad stop. He fell to the ground, exhausted and wet to the core from slogging through the rainforest, swimming across rivers and streams, and narrowly avoiding deadly encounters with jaguars and other predators. Diego sneaked aboard a freight train and rode it down the mountains all the way to the end of the line, Puerto Cortés, on the northern Caribbean coast of Honduras. As far away from the Nicaraguan border as he could get.

He found work on one of the local banana plantations that had finally recovered from the devastation of Hurricane Fifi three years earlier. This time, though, Diego was hired as a truck driver. No one asked for a driver's license. He hauled green bananas from the plantation to Puerto Cortés, where they were transferred to refrigerated containers and shipped all over the world. Driving a beat-up old truck with a reluctant transmission proved a challenge, but it was a whole lot easier and paid much better than picking.

Diego made the one-hour trip between the plantation and the port several times a day, his final run ending in Puerto Cortés in the evening. He stayed in a local hotel and set out before dawn each morning to pick up a new load of freshly harvested bananas. Staying in town and frequenting local cantinas allowed Diego, for the first time in many years, to become friendly with people who didn't exhaust themselves in the fields every day and drink themselves into a stupor every night.

XVIII

In Puerto Cortés, Diego quickly became aware of the recent influx of Americans and British to that thriving port city. This created a growing need for people who could teach Spanish to the children of English-speaking diplomats and shipping executives. Tutors made a hell of a lot more money and suffered a lot less physical stress than truck drivers.

Diego heard from one of the other drivers that businesses in Puerto Cortés were so desperate for Spanish tutor that they were willing to waive the birth certificate requirement. By now, contact with Americans no longer frightened him. Given his sun-weathered face and full beard, he didn't look much like the Braden Delaney anyone might have seen in the newspapers, TV, or wanted posters more than eight years ago.

As soon as the banana harvest ended, he arranged an interview with one of the top tutoring companies in Puerto Cortés. Diego's exposure to Spanish had taught him the cruder dialect spoken by uneducated laborers and farmers, and his accent was distinctly Honduran. But Diego's command of English, which he now made sure he spoke with a hint of an accent, greatly impressed the interviewer. He was hired immediately.

Tutoring was a year-round position, and, for the first time since he arrived in Central America, Diego would be staying in the same place longer than a single harvest season. He hoped he'd been away from the States long enough for the U.S. authorities to have written him off as dead. Even so, he maintained a low profile. He knew it was the careless who got caught.

Being a tutor meant a major step up in Honduran society for Diego. He dressed well, stayed clean all day, and ate better, more civilized meals. At first, he missed the camaraderie that came with his life as a *migratorio,* but the longer he stayed in Puerto Cortés, the more interaction he had with the locals—and not just the spoiled rich children he tutored. At night, though, alone in his two-room apartment, he was gradually losing his battle against mounting depression.

Part of his sadness was due to the fact he saw *himself* in the pampered rich students he tutored. He, too, had attended the expensive private schools open only to the children of families of means. Like his students, he had once assumed that he was better than those who didn't travel in the same social circles. And that included teachers and administrators. He had taken his life of privilege for granted. And look where that had gotten him. Now he'd seen the other side, living in the poverty and squalor of the migrant camps, being treated as part of the expendable flotsam of society. He would never look at the United States, or its citizens, the same way again.

It was neither his place nor his inclination to try to alter the worldview of his arrogant young charges, but he did manage to make the occasional suggestion that there might be merit even in those people who were forced to live in poverty. He couldn't be sure if any of those comments ever took hold.

Diego joined the large raucous crowds at the local *beisbol* stadium to watch the Puerto Cortés ballclub play teams from other towns. He missed playing ball, and when a drinking buddy suggested that they both try out for the local squad, Diego jumped at the chance.

He made the team and got into a few games in left field, but mostly he sat on the bench. The manager was a gruff ex-catcher who liked to maintain the status quo. But when the starting third baseman broke his ankle sliding into home, Diego got his chance. Even though he'd been away from the game for more than eight years, his reflexes were still quick, so he had no trouble fielding, and after a slow start at the plate, he began to get his timing back. As his first season drew to a close, the manager took him aside and told him that he would be Puerto Cortés's third baseman next season; he'd move the former third baseman over to first to take the strain off his repaired ankle. Diego was fitting in nicely.

XIX

It was early in the fall of 1978 when Diego met Elena Valverde at a social gathering of educators. She taught history at Franklin Delano Roosevelt High School, a semiprivate institution—the government paid part of the tuition, but the parents had to come up with the rest. Elena was a rarity among Honduran women in those days—beautiful, well-educated, and independent, dedicated to improving the plight of the Honduran poor.

Diego was taken with her immediately, and he and Elena dated exclusively for nearly three months, during which time Elena proved to be as enlightened in her approach to intimacy as she was in her push for political and social equality. For the first time since he'd arrived in Central America, Diego was emotionally involved. He'd never forget Cheryl Stevens, but that part of his life was gone, never to be recaptured. He'd given up hope that he'd ever see the United States again.

No one was surprised when Elena joined the Roosevelt students who took to the streets demanding a tuition-free education for all. Diego sympathized with the uprising; after all, he'd had some personal experience with student protests. But his reluctance to join Elena on the picket lines effectively ended their relationship. He couldn't tell her the truth, that if he was arrested and fingerprinted, he'd be exposed as a fugitive wanted for murder in the U.S.

Puerto Cortés was a key port that accounted for a major portion of the country's exports, and when the student protestors took over the main streets leading out of the city, it effectively paralyzed the Honduran economy.

The authorities ordered the army to intervene, resulting in several protestors being injured. Elena, who had already been labeled a rebellious troublemaker, was singled out for the worst of the beatings, resulting in a broken leg and wrist, and significant internal damage. She was taken to a prison hospital, where she was promptly neglected.

The military succeeded in forcing the streets of Puerto Cortés to reopen, but in the end, the students got their wish—FDR High School became a free public school.

Officials claimed that radical adults—labeled anti-government insurgents—had orchestrated the protests. They named Elena Valverde as one of the key instigators.

Some of the students tried to go public to set the record straight. But the newspapers operated under the thumb of local politicians, and the efforts of the students went unreported. This all felt eerily familiar to Diego.

The doctors at the prison hospital provided Elena with casts for her leg and wrist but did little to fix the internal bleeding. Diego visited her each of the three days in the hospital before she passed away. He was left heartbroken, angry, and guilt-ridden. But he knew that, as Elena's ex-boyfriend, he would soon be brought in for questioning.

Diego couldn't take the chance they'd learn his true identity. He saw no other choice but to go back on the run. For the first time in many years, he felt more like Braden Delaney than Diego Alcázar.

So, as soon as the term ended, Diego resigned his tutorship, packed his belongings, retrieved all the lempira he had ferreted away, and traded it for pesos. Then he bought his way onto *El Ángel del Mar*, a supply ship heading for Veracruz, Mexico on the shores of the Gulf, with a load of Honduran bananas and livestock. Diego was twenty-nine years old; he'd been in Honduras for almost a decade.

Chapter 12

XX

At midnight on his first day in port, Diego strolled away from the ship. For a fee, Gustavo Garcia, the captain of *El Ángel del Mar*, promised not to give him away if he were questioned. Whether or not Garcia would keep that promise was debatable.

Sneaking to Veracruz was one thing; staying there was another. Diego had no visa and couldn't apply for one since it could lead straight to his true identity. Notwithstanding that problem, Diego figured he had a good chance of disappearing in Veracruz's purported active populace and rowdy nightlife. But even if he managed to pull that off, he would still be a fugitive. He would *always* be a fugitive.

He rented a cheap two-room apartment in the older part of town, but after three weeks, he'd had no luck finding any kind of job—no visa meant no work permit. By limiting himself to two small meals a day, he managed to slow the steady erosion of his funds.

XXI

Diego sat at a window table at Delmar, a popular local seafood restaurant, nursing a cup of coffee. Part of the appeal of Delmar was its free-refills policy. An important perk, since the only thing he could afford at the moment was in the cup in front of him. He spent most mornings here, probing the classifieds in the local newspaper. But he had to admit his hope of finding work was all but dead. He felt like he had only two choices, moving on or a life of crime.

Diego chuckled to himself when he noticed a middle-aged American couple two tables away. Obviously, man and wife. They even dressed alike—red flower-laden shirts and khaki walking shorts. After much frustration with the language barrier, they had managed to order lunch.

The waiter served the couple and started back to the kitchen.

The husband waved impatiently for the waiter to return to their table. "Not so fast there, amigo." He spoke loudly as if the waiter might be hard of hearing, "Mah wife cain't eat this crap. Ah said *no* ... goddamn ... peppahs." He held up a small book titled *Common Spanish Phrases* and jabbed his finger a few times at an entry. "See, it's right here. Just like ah tole you ... no *pimentah!*"

The waiter shrugged. "*Si, señor. No pimienta.* No es pepper." He gestured to the dish in front of the guy's wife and pantomimed using a peppermill.

"What the hell d'ya call this, then?" He jabbed a piece of red bell pepper with his fork and held it up in front of the waiter's face.

The waiter shrugged and threw his arms out to the side.

By now, the other patrons in the restaurant had become an audience.

The American turned red. "Jesus H. Christ, don't any of y'all speak *American*? What the hell kinda place *is* this?"

Diego stood and strode calmly over to the couple's table. He yearned to say: "You're in Mexico, dipshit; it's a Spanish-speaking country." Instead, he said, in English, "Perhaps, I can help." He held out his hand. "I'm Diego Alcázar."

The American gave him a suspicious look but shook his hand. "Ernie Gross."

"It's a simple misunderstanding, Mr. Gross. When you said 'no pimentah,' the waiter thought you were trying to say *pimienta*, which can mean black pepper, the spice. The word for bell pepper is *pimiento*, with an 'o'." He leaned toward the waiter and explained the misunderstanding.

The waiter bowed to Diego and sighed. "*Ah, ahora entiendo. Muchas gracias, señor.*"

Diego nodded to the American couple. "He understands the problem, now."

"Yeah? Well, 'pimentah' is exactly what ah tole him. Ah, cain't help it if he don't understand his own damn language." Gross gestured to the plates in front of them. "Whatever. We ain't eatin' *this* crap."

The restaurant manager rushed to the table. He held his hands up as if he were surrendering. *"Por favor, señor y señora*, ees our playsure *para preparar* a new meal … *correctamente, para ustedes."*

Gross's glare at Diego demanded a translation.

"They'll prepare you a new meal. This time without bell peppers."

Gross shrugged. "Yeah? Well, I ain't paying for it. Not after all this hassle."

Diego relayed that to the manager, who addressed the American with a smile. "S*e cobrará ningún cargo."*

Gross rolled his eyes.

Diego kept it simple. "They'll comp your meal."

Gross flopped back into his chair. "Okay, but they better make it snappy."

"¿Rápido?" Diego asked the manager.

"Sí, sí." The manager gestured for the waiter to hurry. Then he bowed to the Grosses and backed away.

"Thanks for the help, Alcayzer." Gross nodded to Diego.

"De nada." Diego strode back to his own table.

He'd taken only a couple of steps when he heard Mrs. Gross comment, "Well, how do ya like that? He din't even bothah to say, 'You're welcome.' Even when these Mexicans speak American, they's just downright *rude*."

Immediately the waiter refilled Diego's coffee cup and told him to select anything from the menu, and they'd prepare it for him *gratis*. He thanked the waiter and ordered the house specialty, red snapper with tomatoes … and bell peppers. He enjoyed the meal even more given the irony of his selection.

Diego took his time eating, savoring every bite of the first real meal he'd had in days. As he did so, a well-dressed, attractive forty-something woman stopped at his table and handed him her business card. She said in perfect English, "I like the way you defused that situation. I might be able to use someone like you. If you're interested in a job, come by and see me." She pivoted on her heel and left the restaurant without waiting for a reply.

Diego glanced at the card. It was all in Spanish, but he easily translated it: Specialty Exports: Authentic Mexican Art. The name on the card was Anita Ortega, President, the address just a few blocks away.

103

◆ ◆ ◆

I leaned back in the chair and tried to work the kinks out of my lower back. I'd been bent over the manuscript too long. I set the page aside and headed to the kitchenette, poured the remaining coffee from the pot into my mug, and nuked it in the microwave.

I gathered the remaining pages and took them over to the comfortable, overstuffed chair in front of the television. Sore back or not, no way I was stopping now. I took a swig, set the mug on the coffee table, and thumbed through the pages in my hand. Twenty-two handwritten pages left. Braden/Diego's journey would be over soon, and I still had no clue how it would end.

Chapter 13

When Diego walked into Anita Ortega's office, she stood up from her desk and walked over to greet him in English. "As you know from my card, I'm Anita Ortega." She offered her hand.

He shook it. "Yes, I saw that. My—"

"You're Diego Alcázar."

"How did—"

"You introduced yourself to those ill-mannered tourists. But I already knew who you were." She looked him in the eye. "I make it a point to keep track of who's coming and going around here." She motioned him to a tan leather couch against the wall and sat in a matching chair facing him. "As the sign on the door indicates, I'm in the export business."

Diego nodded.

"I specialize in buying traditional Mexican pottery and other crafts from local artisans who still work in the old ways. My customers are wholesalers in the U.S., who ship them all over the world."

He glanced around the nicely appointed office. "And you seem to be doing pretty well."

"Yes, it's become a successful enough one-person business. But I'm on the verge of a small expansion. The demand for my products is increasing, and I'm thinking of hiring someone to help out."

He leaned in closer, gently bit his lip.

"So, I need someone fluent in both Spanish and English." She looked him over. "I thought you might be a good candidate."

Diego cleared his throat, winced. "I'm not sure I—"

She held up her hand, raised an eyebrow. "Are you telling me the young man I see sitting in the Delmar nearly every morning looking through the want ads *isn't* interested in a job?"

"Well, it certainly sounds like the perfect opportunity for me." Diego studied a large cactus plant in the corner. "But I'm afraid you might change your mind."

She raised an eyebrow.

"I don't have a Mexican work permit. I don't even have a visa."

She steepled her fingers and patted them against her chin. "That could be a problem ... but not an insurmountable one. Can I trust you?"

"I assure you I'm honest."

"*Are* you?" She narrowed her eyes at him. "So, Diego Alcázar, are you interested in working for me?"

"Oh yeah. But what about the work permit?"

"It's none of my business why you don't have a visa or a permit. But if you know the right people and are willing to pay, it's possible to obtain the documentation you need ... without enduring the endless red tape and having to deal with inept government officials."

Diego sucked in a breath through clenched teeth. "But I'm afraid I don't know many people here yet, and I doubt I have enough money to—"

"Don't worry, I do." Wry smile.

"Really? That'd be great. I'll pay you back as soon as I save enough pesos."

She nodded. "Yes, you will. I'll be taking it out of your pay." She stood, stepped over to her desk. "Speaking of pay." She grabbed a pen, wrote something on a pad of paper, tore off the top sheet, and handed it to him. "Would this be acceptable to you?"

Diego's eyes widened. It was a lot more than he'd even made tutoring. "Looks good to me."

"If this works out, there may be bonuses, and I'll raise your pay regularly." She smiled, sat at her desk, and picked up the pen again. "Okay, now let's get your details."

Diego handed over his fake Honduran identity papers, from which she copied information. When she finished, Anita looked up at him. "So, you're Honduran."

"Well, let's just say I've spent several years there."

"But your English is so much better than your Spanish." She tilted her head to the side and smiled. "Just how do you explain that?"

"Well, I—"

She waved away his response and laughed. "Around here you are whoever you say you are … *Diego*. Look, as long as your work for me is done discreetly, and you manage to avoid attracting unnecessary attention, we'll get along just fine. But you'll have to do something about that Honduran accent. Mexicans will recognize that whine in your voice right away and trust me, Mexicans don't look kindly on Hondurans."

"Why not?"

"Long story. Let's just say Mexicans don't have much love for *any* Central Americans. Point is, you'll need to work on developing a Mexican accent just to blend in … and to be safe."

"You sound almost like a native English speaker yourself. So how—"

Anita pointed to a framed diploma from the University of Arizona on the wall. "I spent some time in the States. And I met someone. When I graduated, I stayed there for five more years … until my marriage ended."

"Oh, I'm sorry it didn't—"

"I'm not. He was a nice enough guy, but he had a wandering eye. On the other hand, he had plenty of money. It was a tradeoff. I made out just fine in the end."

"So, then Ortega is your maiden name?"

She grinned. "Something like that. As I said, identity here is a fluid thing."

Chapter 14

For six years, Diego traveled rural Mexico, working for Anita. He sought out and purchased authentic native art objects and brought them to Veracruz to be packaged and shipped. The job required long hours and spending some nights in hovels in remote mountain areas. Nothing he couldn't handle. He'd slept in far worse places.

He learned quickly how to recognize quality over quantity—authenticity over forgery—and how to estimate the market value of the earthenware art. In time, he earned the respect of the native artists.

It came as no surprise to Diego that some aspects of Anita's business were a little shady. Anita provided no details, but he suspected some of the artifacts they shipped contained contraband. Probably drugs. He didn't question why the work of certain artisans was handled only by Anita. Diego understood the danger of being arrested and identified by law enforcement, but he'd also seen that Anita had a special relationship with local police. Besides, he trusted her. Who was he to judge anyway? He might now be Diego Alcázar—upstanding Mexican citizen, with the papers to prove it—but beneath the façade, he was still Braden Delaney, a wanted criminal. A murderer.

Once on a rare day off, he visited the library at *La Universidad Veracruzana* to see if he could find anything about Cheryl Stevens. He figured she might be a renowned concert pianist by now. After two hours looking through microfiche, he skimmed several recent English-language newspapers from the States, but he found nothing on Cheryl Stevens there either. Most likely, his earlier speculation was right. Cheryl had probably dropped out of sight, gotten married, and changed her name. In any case, she didn't need him to disrupt her life or her family. Long ago he'd decided it would be best to leave the past buried. He needed to heed his own advice.

Whatever his future might turn out to be, it wouldn't include Cheryl Stevens.

He made good money, and by now tall stacks of five-hundred-peso bills lay hidden under the floorboards in his new two-bedroom apartment. Even in Veracruz, bankers asked too many questions.

Soon enough Diego established himself as a quiet, friendly hombre who made no trouble for anyone. Now something of a regular at local cafés and bars, he'd become fairly popular in Veracruz, especially with the local girls. Most of his relationships with women were pleasant but casual—at least to Diego.

In fact, one of his sometime girlfriends, Mercedes Reyes, claimed she was pregnant by him, and two of her brothers showed up at Diego's door demanding that he marry her. He knew it was unlikely he could be the father of her baby, he always used condoms. Besides he didn't want to marry someone he didn't even like that much, much less love. In the end, Mercedes admitted to her family and Diego that she had never been pregnant. She desperately wanted to force him to marry her because: "*Te quiero tanto.*" I love you so much. Mercedes pleaded

113

with him to forgive her, which he did. Her family, however, didn't let her off so easily. Last he heard, Mercedes had been stuck away in a convent somewhere near Mexico City.

Diego worked hard to shed his Honduran accent and idioms, and soon enough he sounded almost like a native Mexican. He never told anyone he was Honduran. Of course, he *wasn't* Honduran. He wasn't Mexican either. He wasn't even Diego Alcázar.

No matter how comfortably he'd acclimated himself into Veracruz society, he still missed the U.S. It was 1985. He'd been away more than a decade and a half. He'd spent the prime of his life on the run, and he was worn out. But even if there were some way to go back, it would be much too dangerous to return as Braden Delaney. That name and that person would have to stay lost forever.

XXIV

Diego sat at his desk at Specialty Imports staring out the front window.

Anita ended her phone call and glanced over at him. She cleared her throat.

Diego blinked but didn't respond.

"Okay, want to tell me what's going on?"

Diego shrugged, squared a stack of invoices on his desk. "What makes you think something's going on?"

"Come on, sweetie, you've been walking around with that sad puppy face for days. Truth is, Diego, you're starting to get on my nerves." She laughed.

He smiled. "Sorry. Forget it. It's nothing really."

"Don't tell me you've got more girl troubles."

"Nah, it's just that. It's ... well, you know, I've just been thinking about home is all."

She pursed her lips, studied him. "How long has it been?"

"Fifteen years ... so far." He eased out a sigh.

"Are you telling me, after all this time, you're suddenly pining to get back to the U.S.?"

He met her gaze. "I don't know. Not really. I mean I fit in here fine. I love the traveling and working with you feels ... comfortable."

"But?" She raised an eyebrow.

"I dunno. It's just that … well, I'm still an outsider, even here. I guess I just miss home." He squeezed his eyes shut. "I just don't like the idea of growing old in exile."

"Growing old?" She grinned. "Jesus, what are you, thirty-five?

"Next thing I know I'll be forty. Then—"

"Okay, I get it." Anita shook her head, chuckled. "So, what makes you think it would be safe for you to return? Something changed?"

"Not that I know of, but enough time might have passed. By now, maybe they've quit looking for—"

She held up her hand like a stop sign. "I don't need to know the details. I've always assumed you'd gotten yourself into some kind of trouble back in the States. Enough said."

"I hope it wasn't that obvious to everyone."

She gave him a dismissive wave. "So, when were you thinking of trying to slip back in? If you're really serious about it."

"If I do it, I'd want to go soon." He shrugged, gave her a smile. "I mean as soon as you can find a replacement for me. I keep wondering what kind of life I could make for myself back home. Keeps eating at me."

She stood up, stepped over to his desk, and pulled him up into a tight embrace. "It's been a great six-year run, Diego. You've kind of grown on me, you know?" She pulled back and looked him in the eye. "I'm going to miss you. But if this is really what you feel you need to do, I'll help you as much as I can."

He took in a quick breath. "That'd be great. But are you sure you want to be involved?"

She stared into the distance. Diego knew that look. He could almost hear the wheels turning in her brain. He also recognized the half-smile forming at the corner of her mouth.

She strode back to her desk, dropped into the chair, and grabbed a notepad. "Let's see. You'll need a whole new identity—birth certificate, social security card, driver's license, passport … the works. Even a bit of back-story, like a high school diploma and some authentic-looking work history that can't be traced." She looked up at him. "You're going to have to be damn careful you don't ever get yourself fingerprinted for *any* reason. My contacts are experts at this, and they can do a hell of a lot, but they can't alter your prints."

"Trust me, I'll stay far away from anything that looks even *remotely* like trouble."

She locked eyes with him. "It's not just a matter of avoiding arrest, Diego. You won't be able to teach school, for instance. Or coach kids. They might run your prints even for that."

"I understand." Diego nodded. "Um, how much will all that cost?" He cringed. "I've put some money away, but I don't—"

She scoffed. "I'll take care of getting you a new identity. Think of it as a going-away present. I can call in a few favors. How about we fix it so you can go in"—she dragged a bright coral fingernail across her desk calendar—"say, three months? After the first of the year. That should give me time to set everything up."

"Listen, I really appreciate—"

"*De nada.* Besides, I'm going to give you a chance to return the favor."

"Sure, anything."

She grinned. "I knew I could count on you. Here's the deal. One of my colleagues in Texas is out of circulation for a while. I need you to take his place for the January delivery."

Diego knew better than to probe for details.

She eyed him up and down, absently biting her lip. "Now, let's see … I'd say it's time to shave that beard and get a haircut." She grinned. "You don't want to look so much like a *bandito* in your new ID photo. And we'll need to get you a new name. "Diego Alcázar" has a history down here, and it can be traced. And it's way too Hispanic if you're planning to become a *gringo* again."

"Yeah, I know. I'll have to come up with an American name that doesn't call too much attention to itself. I hope to find a place to settle off the grid. You know, fit in but stay virtually invisible to the outside world."

Chapter 15

XXV

Three months later, Diego and Anita were on the road north from Veracruz to Chihuahua in a van carrying several sealed wooden crates that contained the work of a single indigenous pottery maker—Santiago Diaz. In the six years Diego had worked for Anita, he'd never visited Diaz. Diego had never asked why.

Little by little, to avoid suspicion, he'd exchanged his large cache of pesos for U.S. dollars at different banks in and around Veracruz, and now he had nearly five thousand dollars tucked away in the money belt beneath his shirt. He chuckled to himself. Not a lot, but almost the same amount that bastard Lobo had stolen from him all those years ago. Anita slipped him another five grand, calling it a belated Christmas bonus.

The first part of the plan called for loading the crates onto a Cessna 172, and for Diego to accompany the cargo to a remote area in west Texas. The plane touched down on a small dirt strip at an abandoned farm near Van Horn well after sunset. Diego and the pilot loaded the crates into several secret compartments built into a well-used 1978 Volkswagen camper. He couldn't help but smile at the coincidence. This was a newer version of the VW bus in which he'd escaped to Sadie's Farm so many years ago. Things were coming full circle.

Despite the look of the camper's exterior, he was assured the engine was in prime condition; given the cargo, a breakdown on the road could prove disastrous. The inside of the camper appeared to be fully equipped, but most of the cabinets and appliances were false fronts to secret compartments for hiding the crates.

Following the second part of the plan, Diego drove the van five and a half hours straight to Las Cruces, New Mexico, then west to Safford, a few miles inside the eastern border of Arizona. All the while keeping well away from the U.S.-Mexican border.

A room had already been reserved for him at a small motel just outside town. He arrived a little after eight in the evening, but the motel manager had been alerted he'd be making a late check-in. He locked the camper and engaged the van's elaborate anti-theft system.

The room had been paid for in advance, so he had no trouble slipping away from the motel at dawn the next morning as instructed. When he reached Winslow, Arizona, he traveled to a strip mall at the edge of town. Following the plan, he drove the camper around to the back and parked it in the designated spot near the back door of Carlotta's Authentic Mexican Cuisine. Again, he locked the camper and set the alarm system. Then he headed off on foot, and once he'd put a mile between himself and the strip mall, he buried the keys in a random trash receptacle.

He spent the next night in a cheap motel near a seedy used car dealership. As soon as the lot opened in the morning, he marched over and, after some haggling, bought a 1968 Ford pickup for six hundred dollars. The body needed work, but the engine appeared to be in pretty good shape.

He drove the pickup west through Arizona into California. It was 1986; he was thirty-six years old. He'd left Diego Alcázar behind, and Braden Delaney was a distant, fading memory. His experiences in Central America and Mexico had made him a lot older and, he hoped, much wiser than when he'd left the U.S.

He planned to seek out a small town in a remote part of the state, where he could settle in quietly and remain under the radar for the rest of his life. He was through with his past and now more than ready for whatever life might throw his way.

I turned over the last page and wiped my eyes. I felt like I'd been sitting at Dad's feet, listening to him tell the story. Just like when I was a kid.

I carried the pages back to the desk and set them down on top of the others. It took me a minute to identify my feelings. Then I caught a glimpse of my beaming reflection in the apartment window.

What I felt was pride. I was proud of Dad for having written such a remarkable story and just as proud that *I* was the one he chose to read it.

Chapter 16

To say the least, I was captivated by Dad's novel. Hell, I'd have been impressed no matter who wrote it. Okay, so his tale of Braden Delaney was yet another take on the coming-of-age tale. But not so many of those novels depicted a protagonist who had to answer for youthful indiscretions by spending his best years in exile. And I liked the hopeful, open-ended finish.

Since he was something of a spoiled rich kid, "Braden Delaney" felt like a great name for Dad's protagonist. And he set up perfectly logical circumstances that led Delaney to adopt the name Diego Alcázar. He could easily have picked a more common Hispanic surname for Delaney's alias, but instead, he chose Alcázar. Exotic for sure, and according to the narrative, an old *Spanish* surname, not Honduran. I've been told I go a little overboard with character-naming in my short stories. I often gave characters names with deeper meanings—like Blight and Kostick. Had Dad done something like that here?

I'd guessed "Diego" translated to "David" in English, but when I consulted an online Spanish-English dictionary, I discovered "Diego" was actually a diminutive form of Santiago—Spanish for "Saint James." "Alcázar," it turned out, originated with the Moors of Spain, and the name meant citadel, royal place … castle.

So, when I translated Diego Alcázar, I got James Castle. I got *Dad*.

I tried to take a deep breath, coughed instead. Then I chuckled. A surprise for sure, but a well-established technique. So, Dad subtly put his own name in his novel. Why not? Other authors have done it. And Dad was not nearly as blatant as Stephen King, who put a character named "Stephen King" into *The Dark Tower* series. Made me smile. No reason James Castle couldn't do the same thing. Not only that, who's to say Dad didn't translate his own name to Spanish, figure out a way to insert it into his novel, and create the rationale behind it afterward? Pretty damn clever. I broke into a broad grin, shook my head. That Dad.

But my smile slowly faded. What if the story of Braden Delaney wasn't fiction at all? What if it was a retelling of Dad's life before he showed up in California? We knew next to nothing about his past.

My spine turned to ice; my whole body went numb. Had he been living under the false name "Jim Castle" all this time? In a lot of ways, the manuscript *did* read more like a memoir than fiction. Except if it was a memoir, why write it in the third person? Then again, no reason someone couldn't tell his life story as a novel.

Nope. Couldn't be. Come on, if the story *were* true, it would mean Dad wasn't the man I knew. The man I've always idolized, patterned myself after. The man who *defined* me. I sneered. Right, like Dad could really be someone named Braden Delaney. I knew Jim Castle. I loved Jim Castle. I didn't really know Delaney *at all*.

I paced the apartment, a caged tiger, until I finally came to a conclusion. Dad's novel was just that. Fiction. Period. End of discussion.

It was simply *inconceivable* for Dad to be anything other than the adoring father I'd known so well and loved so unconditionally. Please. It was ridiculous to even consider the possibility that my best friend, my idol, could once have been a criminal. A fugitive. A killer! *Hell* no. I knew Dad too well.

I slumped back into the chair, light-headed, while my stomach battled what was left of my lunch. I wanted to let the whole preposterous idea go. I was exhausted. Yeah, that was it. After all, I'd been staring at those handwritten pages for hours on end. I just needed a break.

I set the final pages on the pile, flipped the stack upright, knocked the sheets in place. I studied the pile for a few seconds, then smoothed out the top sheet with my palm, and placed it all in the bottom drawer of my desk. I'd read it again tomorrow.

Things would look different in the morning.

Chapter 17

My cell phone shocked me out of my senseless mind games. A text from Chelsea Rutledge: *Hi, Babe. I miss you. Ready for some company? I'll come bearing pizza.* Chelsea was the closest thing I had to a girlfriend. Okay, she *was* my girlfriend. Since I returned to Shoat Valley after college, she and I dated exclusively. We hadn't talked much since the funeral; she understood my need to grieve alone.

No, I hadn't finished mourning. Maybe I never would. How was I supposed to get over the loss of the man I'd spent my whole life emulating? But Chelsea had perfect timing. I needed to rejoin the real world, and she might be the perfect person to help me push aside all this ludicrous speculation about Dad's manuscript. I texted her back: *Miss you too. Pizza sounds great. I'll supply the beer. Tonight works for me.*

She texted back: *6:30 then <3*

That cute signoff symbol, which Chelsea included in all her texts to me, meant more to her than just a heart symbol. It was also a mathematical definition—less than three, so two, a couple. Us. Felt a little too confining to me, but not so far from the truth. Be hard to find someone who could outshine Chelsea. I wasn't holding out for something better.

In fact, folks in Shoat Valley were forever telling Chelsea and me that we were the cutest couple in town. Flattering to be sure, but then with the population of the greater Shoat Valley area barely topping a thousand, we didn't have that much competition.

Chelsea was two years younger than me, and we had a lot in common, in the way people who are comfortable living in a small town do. She officially lived with her parents, but until Dad died, she'd spent most nights at my place. She was a smart, attractive blonde with a terrific sense of humor, and sensuous as hell. Perfect, right?

But our relationship was missing something. For me anyway. Don't get me wrong. I felt real affection for Chelsea. I liked spending time with her. We had a lot of fun together. I looked forward to seeing her each day. She was my favorite person in the world outside my family. Hell, she was treated like family by my mom and dad. And she and my sister, Shelby, were best friends.

But I didn't think I loved Chelsea. The thing was, I'd never been in love before, so I didn't have anything to compare it to. I was pretty sure, though, there was supposed to be some sort of spark. Something that you felt from the inside out, something that announced that *this* was the right person. Maybe Chelsea felt it, but I didn't. At least not yet. I'd gotten plenty of hints that she hoped our relationship was following a path that would lead to the altar. Maybe it would.

We had a pleasantly exhausting reunion. From the first, we'd been in sync sexually. It was no fault of hers that my fitful dreams this time were of Braden Delaney, not her. I didn't feel as if I'd slept at all. I was wide awake, staring at the ceiling, when the sun first peeked through the blinds just before 5:00 a.m. Careful not to wake her, I slipped out of bed, pulled on gym shorts, and hunkered down at my desk with Dad's manuscript.

By the time Chelsea woke up, I'd been engrossed in the manuscript for over an hour. I read slowly and carefully, looking for any signs that it might not be a draft of a novel. I was so focused on the manuscript I didn't even notice Chelsea had gotten out of bed.

She eased up and hugged me from behind with her soft, sleep-warm body. "Good morning, Baby."

"Morning," I gasped, as I jammed the pages into a desk drawer as if I'd been caught reading interspecies child porn.

Chelsea didn't question me about it. "I woke up all *lonely*." She pulled me up from the chair into a skin-to-skin embrace. "And I'm not ready to get up yet," she whispered in my ear. Then she led me by the hand back to the bed.

Afterward, we showered, dressed, and shared a breakfast of eggs, bacon, toast, and fresh-brewed coffee. We chatted about everything going on in Shoat Valley. Everything but Dad. By seven we kissed goodbye, and she headed out for her shift as a nurse intern at Mercy Medical over in Mt. Shasta.

Alone again, I shut off the coffee pot, poured the last of the brew into my mug, and plunged back into the story. Then I read it over a third time from the beginning. But the manuscript revealed no answers to the disconcerting questions rattling around in my brain. Was Dad the person who had nurtured me, loved me, and molded me into the man I'd become? Or was he someone else, someone hiding a secret life? Was the name we all knew him by a *lie*? Was *he*?

No … just, no.

I headed out of my apartment and descended the back stairs to Book Castle. Work would hopefully distract me for a while. After I opened the shop, I fired up the espresso machine and made myself a double cappuccino. I took the pink delivery boxes from the Valley Bakery driver, carried them to the counter, and arranged the pasties in the display case. Once I'd taken care of the early morning regulars, I sat down at the desk and booted up the store computer.

As much as I wanted to, though, I couldn't shake my anxiety. If the answers I needed weren't in the story itself, then maybe I'd have luck elsewhere. I googled the Kent State Massacre and followed the thread to articles about the campus turmoil that spread across the country back in the late Sixties and early Seventies. Wikipedia could be suspect, but the details there and in other articles seemed to echo those in Dad's manuscript. He would have been the right age to have been involved in some of the protests himself—or at least to have read about it and seen it on television. And just because he never went to college, that didn't mean he couldn't have been swept up in the anti-war movement.

I searched "Carlyle University." But the school's website didn't tell me anything about 1970. I entered "Carlyle University ROTC bombing," came up empty. Okay, that meant, even though all the stuff about the student protests in the Seventies was based on fact, Dad probably created the story of the bombing out of thin air. Either that or it hadn't been a big enough event to maintain interest over forty years later. Or maybe the college just chose to bury a black mark on its history.

I leaned forward, elbows on the desk, and held my face in my hands … trying to rub away my suspicions, my *doubts* about the man who has meant more to me than anyone else in the world.

The old-fashioned bell over the store entrance tinkled. I looked up and smiled a welcome to Audrey Cartwright, as always resplendent in brightly colored cotton polyester, this time mostly blue. Ms. Cartwright was my history teacher in high school, retired now, who often browsed but rarely bought anything.

As the sweet old woman wandered through the stacks, I did an unsuccessful Google search for "Braden Delaney," which turned up lots of *Brendan* Delaneys, even a few Braden Delaneys, but none of them old enough to have been twenty in 1970. I discovered a whole lot of Cheryl Stevenses; not surprising, it was a common name. All were too young. Tried searching Facebook. Same results.

Googling Cindy Parks, the girl allegedly killed in the fire, resulted in several options, but nothing about one of them dying in an explosion at Carlyle. Found nothing on Diego Alcázar either. On a whim, I even searched for Lobo. When I got past the wolf references, I found a character who once appeared in a DC Comics series. Another dead end.

My stomach flipped. How was all this being fair to Dad? What would he think if he was watching me now? The hair on the back of my neck stiffened.

I looked up into the flushed face of Ms. Cartwright. She set a copy of *Fifty Shades of Grey* face down on the counter.

I gave her a warm smile, one that couldn't be construed as judgmental. "This is one of our most popular titles," I told her, as I rang up her purchase.

"Well … um, I'm curious to see what all the fuss is about," she said without looking me in the eye.

I slipped the book into her tote bag without further comment.

Once she was gone, I did a quick tour of the store, half expecting to see Dad shelving books as I had so often over the years. Not this time.

Despite the sensation that Dad was there, looking over my shoulder, disgusted with my unwarranted suspicions, I dropped back down in front of the computer. I just wanted to get this *research* over with so I could move on from the anxiety I'd foisted upon myself. If I didn't find anything, any evidence, I'd chuck the whole thing and concentrate on getting Dad's novel edited and published.

After several word combinations, I struck out on Sadie's Farm, the Oregon commune near Medford, where Braden Delaney hid for a few days. But even if it had existed back in 1970, I imagined it would have been disbanded long ago, when the hippie movement died and most commune members grew older, got tired of living off the land, and assimilated back into mainstream society as organic gardeners or insurance salesmen.

I tried another approach. Why not search the archives of the largest paper in Washington, the *Seattle Post-Intelligencer*? Should have thought of that earlier. But the PI's online archives went back only as far as 1990. *The Sinclair Gazette*—the local

132

paper in the town where Carlyle University was located—didn't have *any* archives on its website.

I got up, stretched, and made myself another cappuccino. All this wild suspicion—quite possibly boosted by way too much caffeine—was driving me nuts. I wanted to toss my concerns about Dad's manuscript onto the coincidence pile or chalk it all up to creative license. So, why wasn't it that simple?

I glanced at the clock … ten thirty, time for Carla Eisner, from Dream Getaways Travel next door, to pick up her regular morning coffee break order—two lattes, a cappuccino, two blueberry muffins, and a maple-nut scone. I'd just finished topping off the lattes—one with a foam heart, the other with a leaf—when Carla walked in.

Ten minutes later, I held the door for her as she strolled out, the drinks in a cardboard carrier in one hand and a bag of pastries in the other. Then I settled back at the desk. As much as I tried to convince myself I was on a fool's errand, I just couldn't let my fears go. Not yet.

Google produced lots of information on Honduras, and as far as I could tell the details in the manuscript about the terrain and coffee and banana harvests were accurate. Of course, back when he wrote this, Dad could easily have looked all that stuff up in an encyclopedia or something. Same with Hurricane Fifi and the protest by high school students in Puerto Cortés. All research he would have done for the sake of verisimilitude. A lot of work for a rough draft, but certainly commendable.

Unless he experienced it all firsthand. Shit.

All I'd been told about Dad's past was he'd been born in Massachusetts, his parents died when he was young, and he'd graduated from high school in 1968. Okay, that meant he could have been twenty in 1970—same as Braden Delaney. Already knew that.

Other questions started to raise their ugly heads, and I didn't need the Internet to corroborate them. What, for instance, had Dad been doing in the eighteen years between his high school graduation and his arrival in Shoat Valley in 1986?

Maybe the first thing I should have done was write down the characteristics of Braden Delaney and see how many of them matched Dad's. I made a neat two-column list on a notepad and went back through the manuscript.

In the "Braden" column I wrote "intelligent"; under "Dad," "the smartest person I know"—and that included many of my professors at Sonoma State. Braden: "baseball player"; Dad: "softball player." Braden: "hair dark enough he could pass for Hispanic"; Dad: "gray, thinning, but dark in his younger days, like me." Braden: "knew some Spanish"; Dad: "took Spanish in high school."

Okay, so Jim Castle did somewhat resemble the protagonist of his novel. So would hundreds of other guys. I chuckled.

Maybe Mom could shed some light on the swamp of speculation I'd thrown myself into. At least she'd know things about her husband's life before I came along. If I talked with her, I'd have to be careful not to mention anything specific from the manuscript, of course. No way I'd reveal the real reason I was curious. Then again, if I did, she'd probably dismiss it all with a hearty laugh. Then she'd look at me like I was an alien inhabiting her son's body. But maybe I could get her to inadvertently provide some proof that Jim Castle couldn't possibly be Braden Delaney.

I'd stop by and talk to her after Book Castle closed tonight. Maybe then I could just let it go. For now, I welcomed the diversion of inventorying and shelving today's shipments and dealing with the usual afternoon influx of customers.

Chapter 18

I knew the second I opened the door that Mom was baking cookies, chocolate chip. My favorite. I was suddenly a little kid again.

I walked into the kitchen and gave her a hug. When I released her, she rewarded me with a warm smile, something I hadn't seen often since Dad died.

She brushed a strand of blonde hair behind her ear and turned back to arranging the freshly baked cookies on a plate. At forty-eight, she could have passed for ten years younger.

I took a seat at the kitchen table. She set the plate of cookies in the middle and sat across from me. Neither of us took Dad's chair.

She nudged the plate toward me. "Just a little something to go with our coffee, sweetheart. I know they're your favorite."

"*Oh* yeah." I surveyed the selection, picked the biggest one.

She glanced at the empty chair at the head of the table. Chocolate chip cookies were Dad's favorite, too. We didn't have to say it.

I took a bite, savored it. "You make the best chocolate chip cookies in the universe."

She chuckled. "You always were prone to exaggeration, dear." Broad smile. "So, what was it you wanted to discuss?"

"I know it's been tough on you … on all of us, but would you be okay talking about Dad?"

A loving-sad smile formed, then faded. "Of course, honey. But I can't guarantee that I won't get a little emotional."

I nodded, grinned. "No problem. Same goes for me." I paused, still looking her in the eye. "Tell me again how you met Dad?"

"You want to hear *that* old story again?"

"Yeah. I've just been wondering what Dad was like before I knew him, you know? There's a lot about his life that's a blank for me."

"Well, the first time I saw Jim was when I walked into the bookstore. It was called Shoat Valley Books back then. I stopped in to pick up the copy of *The Color Purple* I'd ordered. I'd seen the movie … and I was anxious to read the book. You know how they sometimes make a movie out of a book, and it turns out to be a completely different story?"

"Uh-huh."

137

"Anyway, I wasn't much older than you are now. I was working as a receptionist at the Valley Animal Clinic." She shook her head. "I haven't thought of old Doc Halston for years. Funny little man, but he was a darn good vet. It was my first real job after college. You couldn't do much with a degree in sociology back in those days."

I chuckled. "You still can't, Mom. It's one of those dead-end degrees."

She peered at me over the top of her glasses. "That's pretty smart talk … coming from an English major."

I held my hands up, to let her know she'd won that one. Snatching another cookie, I pulled a napkin from the holder. "You were telling me about the first time you met Dad."

"Oh, right. So, I walked into the bookstore expecting to see old man Whitley sitting behind the counter smoking away on his pipe like always. He'd owned the store forever. But that day Jim Castle stood behind the counter." She paused. "He was the handsomest man I'd ever met. He had the warmest, most sincere smile." She glanced around as if making sure no one else was listening, leaned closer. "I wanted to crawl inside that smile and live there forever."

I nodded.

She stared at me, maybe through me.

"Whaaat?" I shrugged.

"I'm still taken by how much you're turning out to look like him … well, how he must have looked when he was younger. He was thirty-six when I met him. Thing is though, I see *him* every time I look at you." She took in a ragged breath, eased it out. "I'm so thankful for that."

I reached across and placed my hand on top of hers.

She glanced down at our hands. "Um, so where were we, sweetie?"

"You were telling me Dad just showed up in the store one day. You'd think he would have been living in Shoat Valley before that."

She pointed to my mouth, raised an eyebrow.

I wiped the chocolate from my lips with the napkin.

"Maybe, but Dad always said he bought the place with a handshake and a down payment. Kind of sounds like Mr. Whitley too. But, the truth is, I don't *know* exactly when he arrived here, but I *do* know if I'd seen Jim Castle around before that, I sure as heck would have remembered him." She got that faraway look.

Not the time to press her. I waited, took another cookie but set it down on my napkin without taking a bite. Sipped coffee instead.

She turned back to me and blinked, as if startled to see me sitting there.

My cue to continue. "Thing is, I've heard almost everything about Dad's life in Shoat Valley. But I don't know a darn thing about him before he showed up here." I clasped my hands together on the table. "Um ... so he must have talked to you in *private* ... about his past."

She took a breath, hesitated. Then she stood. "Here, let me warm up our coffee."

139

"*I* can get it, Mom." I started to rise.

She waved me back down, padded over to the counter in her stocking feet. She removed her glasses, wiped her eyes with a napkin, and gazed out the kitchen window. She continued with her back to me. "Jim turned that bookstore into a real moneymaker when he added coffee and pastries. People thought he was crazy, but he proved them all wrong."

She was avoiding my question, just as she always had whenever I'd asked her about Dad's past. As a kid, I'd always shrugged it off as "grown-up stuff" that children didn't need to know. But I wasn't a kid anymore, and I *definitely* needed to know.

She replaced her glasses, unplugged the ceramic coffee pot, and brought it to the table. "Book Castle soon became a kind of gathering place. Partly because of the coffee, but I think it was mostly because of Dad's friendly personality. He just naturally drew people to him."

I slid my coffee mug toward her. She topped it off and did the same for hers.

"Yes, he sure did." I took a sip and set my mug back down. "He was a smart businessman for sure. A bit surprising for a guy who never went to college."

"Jim Castle was one of those men who had plenty of smarts without formal education. He always regretted not going, though. That's one reason he was so adamant about you and Shelby getting college degrees—even if it was only in English." She grinned.

140

I returned it. Time to try a different tack. "I'm still confused why our family albums include pictures of us, and you and your sister as kids, even your parents, but there's not one picture of Dad's childhood or his family."

She took a cookie from the plate, placed it in the exact center of the napkin sitting next to her coffee mug, stared it down. "Honey, we've talked about this. We couldn't include photos of Dad or his family, because he never had any. We *told* you that."

"Right. But do you know *why* he didn't have any?"

"He never spelled it out in detail, but whenever I asked him about his childhood, I got the impression there was some sort of falling out between Jim and his parents long ago."

"Are you saying he never told you *anything* about his life before you met? Doesn't that seem a little weird?"

"I asked him all sorts of questions about that stuff when we were first together, but he wouldn't answer them. Even made him angry once. It was our first fight. I avoided the issue after that. He always said that he preferred to leave his past where it belonged—over and done with. And I'm fine with that."

"I understand. But you must have speculated about what happened to Dad before you met him."

"Of course, I did, sweetie. He never mentioned it directly, but it's possible his family life wasn't very happy." She sighed, looked away. "People don't like to talk about unpleasant things."

I pretended I didn't get the hint. "So, do you think something happened to him when he was younger? Abuse, maybe?"

"Don't know." She shook her head. "He never mentioned any. But I suspected something awful had happened to him in the past, and he'd done his best to wash it away. He just didn't want to deal with it anymore. Sometimes I wondered if Jim suffered from a kind of posttraumatic stress disorder."

"Really? I never noticed any signs of PTSD in Dad."

"You wouldn't have, honey. He'd managed to put that all behind him by the time you were born."

"I suppose it makes sense he wouldn't want to revisit his early years if they were that awful. Makes you wonder, though."

"He claimed the past didn't really matter anyway, because he'd never been happier in his life than when he was with us. I saw the evidence of that every day. But you already know that, Nick."

"Yeah. I've never seen a man more devoted to his wife and family than Dad was."

"That's not just devotion, honey. That's love. Real love. He showed it to me in so many ways every day. And I loved him just as much … still do." She looked away, blotted her eyes with a napkin.

I gave her some space. I'd noticed it, too. Dad was totally in love with her and you could see it in the way he studied her when she wasn't looking, in how his eyes lit up whenever she appeared, and in how he held on longer than necessary when he hugged her as if he was just too emotional to let go right away.

Finally, she looked back at me, tilted her head, scrunched up her face. "What makes you so curious about that now?"

"No reason, really." I shrugged. "It's just … there are so many things I don't know about Dad. Now that he's … gone. I've just been thinking about him a lot."

"Me, too, honey … me, too."

We relaxed in silence for a minute, letting the budding tension evaporate.

I nudged the cookie around on the napkin with a finger, then changed the subject. "I guess he must have been a pretty good baseball player when he was younger," I said without looking up.

"Well, as you well know, he was an excellent softball player, even after he had some years on him. When we were first married, some guys from the Bay Area came all the way up here to try to get him to join their softball team. They played tournaments all over the West Coast. They were after him pretty hard, but he turned them down."

"Wow, I never knew that. It was obvious, though, he had a lot more sports knowledge and experience than most of the dads who signed up to coach. Kinda surprising Dad never wanted to coach any of our teams when we were kids."

"I think he just felt more comfortable helping out. You know, not being in charge, staying out of the limelight. He spent plenty of time with you and Shelby individually, though."

I peered over the rim of my steaming cup at Mom, who was lost in her thoughts. I gave her a moment, cradled my warm mug in both hands. Then, I lifted my cup to my lips, and, as if I'd just thought of it, said, "By the way, do you still have Dad's high school diploma stashed away somewhere? I'd like to look at it."

"I sure do. And I know exactly where all that stuff is." She stood up.

"I don't want you to go to any trouble, Mom. I can get it."

"No trouble, sweetie. Be right back."

She reappeared a few minutes later with the diploma and a transcript in hand. "Here you go. Dad would have wanted you to have these … I mean, if you're looking for keepsakes or something."

Gently laying the documents on the table, I patted the top one. "I'll take good care of these, Mom." I glanced at the transcript. "Jeez, with grades like this it seems weird he didn't go to college."

"Maybe it had something to do with that part in of his life he doesn't … didn't like to talk about." Her lower lip quivered; she turned away and wiped her nose with a napkin.

I offered a half-grin and a shift to a lighter topic. "Mom, I don't know if you knew this, but Dad told me once he always wanted to write a novel."

A smile spread across her face. "It doesn't surprise me that he'd think about doing a novel. He loved that *you* were writing. He was very impressed with your short stories."

"Yeah, he thought I should consider becoming a serious writer." I ran my fingers through my hair. "Actually, I've been thinking about maybe … starting to write again."

She tilted her head to the side. "Oh, you should, Nick. He'd like that."

I picked up the documents, stepped over, and gave her a kiss on the cheek. "Thanks, Mom. It was nice being able to talk like this even though I know it wasn't easy for you."

She stood and wrapped her arms around me. I gave her a bear hug, lifted her off the ground, let her go only when she started to giggle. A thing we often did, ever since I'd grown taller than her.

I'd learned little to help me unravel the mystery I'd created—with no real evidence in the first place. Well, Mom did confirm that Dad had a past he wouldn't reveal, and his refusal to coach echoed Anita Ortega's warning to Diego to avoid getting fingerprinted. Circumstantial evidence at best. I waited for the sinking feeling in my stomach to subside. Mom had never really cared about Dad's past. She'd loved him for the life he shared with her, and she always would. So would Shelby. So should I.

♦ ♦ ♦

As much as I wanted to, though, I just couldn't shake my doubts. I *had* to know once and for all that Dad wasn't actually Braden Delaney. Back at my apartment, I checked the internet to see what I could find out about St. Adelaide Academy in Boston, the high school named on Dad's diploma. Turns out it burned to the ground in 1969, all records lost. A coincidence? Or was that exactly the reason St. Adelaide was chosen for a fake transcript and diploma? Untraceable.

I closed my eyes and sat back in the overstuffed chair, my thinking spot. If I hoped to get to the truth, I'd need to start with what happened to the ROTC building on the Carlyle campus in the spring of 1970. The best way to do that was to go to Sinclair, Washington, and wade through microfilm in the university library. If that bombing happened, they'd likely have information on Braden Delaney, too. If he really was the one who blew it up. If anybody did.

But I wasn't kidding myself. If I went to Carlyle, what I really hoped to find was that no one named Braden Delaney ever existed … and that James Castle had never been a student at Carlyle. Once I knew that, none of the rest of it would matter.

A leisurely two-day trip from Northern California might also mellow me out, give me a chance to think things through. Stop creating demons.

According to Google Maps, the best route would be to go straight up I-5 to Medford, just across the Oregon border. That's where Sadie's Farm was supposed to have been. No question that seeing what I could discover in Oregon and Washington would be a hell of a lot better than staying home beating myself over the head with doubt and speculation.

When I told Mom I needed to get away for a while, she understood.

"I'll wait until Shelby's home for the summer," I said. "I don't want you to have to shoulder the load all by yourself."

"Oh *please*, I can take care of things just fine. I'll just ask Janey Grimes to work a few more hours. She'll like that. She can use the extra money."

"You sure?"

She rolled her eyes. "Your sister'll be home in two days, for crying out loud. I'm sure Janey and I can keep the shop afloat 'til then."

I chuckled along with her.

Chapter 19

I tossed my travel bag in the back seat and dropped behind the wheel of my two-year-old Prius. Then I called Chelsea to let her know I'd be out of town for a few days. Turned out to be a longer conversation than I anticipated.

"Oh, Nick, if you had told me you were going, I could have gotten time off work. I could have gone with you."

"Sorry, it wasn't something I planned. Kinda spur of the moment, you know?"

"So, you didn't want me to go with you in the first place."

"Well, I … I just need to be on my own for a while … to sort out my feelings about the loss of Dad."

"Sure. Of course. But … *we're* okay, right?"

"Sure, same as we've always been." I never handle situations like this well.

"Are you saying our relationship is *boring*?"

I rubbed my forehead. The last thing I wanted to do was upset her. "No, Chelsea, that's not what I'm saying at all."

Huge sigh. "I … I'm sorry, Babe. It's just that … you've been pretty inaccessible since Jim died, and … well, it hasn't been easy for me either. I miss spending time with you. I miss *us*."

"Look, you know things have been crazy for me since it happened ... and I'm hoping this trip will help me find my way back to normal."

The line fell silent long enough for me to wonder if we'd lost our connection.

Then I heard her take a ragged breath on the other end. Finally, she said, "See you when you get back then."

"Yep, I'm planning to be gone no more than a few days."

We hung up. Like I didn't already have enough emotional turmoil bouncing around in my brain like lottery balls in a wire basket.

I headed out of the driveway. I'd try to put Chelsea's mind at ease when I got back.

♦ ♦ ♦

So, I didn't get on the road until almost ten, and it was just after eleven-thirty when I passed the first Medford exit. Time to stretch my legs and grab an early lunch. Then again, Medford might have much more to offer than a bite to eat. Stopping there could also be a chance to find out if a commune or *anything* around there had once been called Sadie's Farm. A long shot.

At Hogan's Gyros, a sandwich shop in the middle of town, I picked up a hot pastrami-and-swiss sub and a Coke. The pretty brunette at the counter with an elaborate peacock tattoo on her shoulder gave me a blank stare when I asked her if she'd ever heard of Sadie's Farm. Much too young. But she did know of a nice place to relax while I ate—Alba Park, just a block away.

I took my lunch over to the park and found a small picnic area. Off to one side, a group of teens was texting and sharing a joint. The only other people I saw were two old men, a few tables away. They were playing what looked, strangely enough, like Battleship. I was surprised that the game still existed.

The high school kids wouldn't likely know anything about a commune that may or may not have existed twenty-five years before they were born. So, I picked a table near the old guys and ate. It *was* Battleship.

I listen to the coded conversation, which seemed to be building momentum.

One of them, bald, in a blue work shirt with ragged cuffs, said, "B-8."

The other one, in a faded green baseball cap, with a full white beard, laughed. "Hah. You miss! I'm gunning for G-4."

Blue Shirt scrunched up his face. "Hit. Damn it."

Green Cap yanked the hat from his shiny dome and slapped the table with it. "No need to keep playing. I know exactly where your battleship is. It's as good as sunk!"

Blue Shirt stared at the game board. "You're just about the luckiest son of a bitch I ever saw."

"Lucky, hell! I just pay more attention than you."

Blue Shirt shrugged. "If you say so." He made a mark on a notepad next to the game board. "That makes us tied for the day."

"Told you I'd catch up." Green Cap chuckled. "Quit stallin'. I'm on a hot streak. Get your damn boats back on the water so I can whip your ass again."

150

I dropped the sandwich wrapper into a nearby bin and strolled over. "Excuse me. I don't mean to interrupt your game, but I was hoping you might be able to help me out."

Both men narrowed their eyes at me.

I gave them my best non-threatening smile. "No, no. I'm not looking for a handout … just some information."

Blue Shirt raised an eyebrow. "What kinda information you lookin' for, son?"

"I'm hoping that one of you might have lived around here back in the early Seventies."

Green Cap grinned. "Thanks for the compliment, son, but I'm afraid neither one of us'll see our early seventies again."

"He's not talking about your age, you deaf ol' gaffer." Blue Shirt rolled his eyes. "He wants to know about the *nineteen*-seventies."

Green Cap shrugged. "Well anyway, you came to the right place. I've lived here every one of my eighty-two years." He motioned for me to sit down at the table next to him.

"I've lived in Medford since 1955," Blue Shirt said. "Moved here to go to work for Harry and David. They're the biggest mail-order fruit marketer in the whole damn country, you know. Worked there more'n forty years."

I nodded. "Oh yeah, I've heard of—"

"He ain't interested in your goddamn career packagin' fruits and nuts." Green Cap snorted. He turned to me. "What is it you're lookin' to find out, son?"

"Well, I was wondering if either of you has ever heard of a commune that was supposed to be near Medford around 1970?"

"What's a commune?" Green Cap asked.

151

Blue Shirt scoffed. "You know, one of them hippie places back then where everybody lived like one big family. They was tryin' to be all *organic* or some such. Named their kids shit like 'Rainbow' and 'Morning Glory.'"

"Oh yeah." Green Cap nodded. "I remember now. Those hippies set them things up so they could get away from all the laws the rest of us had to go by." He leaned in toward me. "They had sex whenever they damn well felt like it, with anyone they wanted to, is what I heard."

"I could go for that." Blue Shirt grinned.

Green Cap scoffed. "In your dreams."

"I was hoping one of you might remember a particular commune called Sadie's Farm."

Green Cap scrunched up his face. "Ladies Arm? That's the stupidest—"

"No, no, you dried up ol' prune pit, he said *Sadie's Farm*," Blue Shirt shouted. "Turn up your hearing aid, for Christ's sake."

"Jesus quit yer damn yellin'," Green Cap said. "Don't need to turn it up to listen to your babbling. I hear jess fine."

Blue Shirt rolled his eyes. "Yeah, we can see that."

I tried again. "Umm, so *have* either of you heard of Sadie's Farm?"

Green Cap scratched the stubble on his chin. "Well, lemme see. Yeah, I think there was one of them hippie places around here back then. They *acted* like farmers. Grew their own vegetables, as I recall."

"Most of them hippies got themselves in big trouble for growing illegal vegetables," Blue Shirt added with a wink.

Green Cap tilted his head to the side and scrunched up his mouth. "Seems to me the cops was always raiding those places. Looking for any damn excuse to arrest somebody. Them hippies never got along with the cops."

I took a deep breath. "Okay, so about Sadie's Farm. Do you think there might have been a local commune called that?"

"I recall there was some a them around here back then. But I can't say for *sure* if any of 'em was the place you're talkin' about," Green Cap said.

Blue Shirt nodded. "Coulda been Sadie's Farm, I s'pose."

Green Cap grinned at his companion. "Hell, coulda been damn near *anything*. You can't even remember what happened last week, much less way the hell back in nineteen and seventy."

Blue Shirt glared at him. "Well it *coulda* been that place he's talkin' about. You don't know it wasn't."

I stood up to go. "Well, thanks. I really appreciate your trying to help me out."

As I strolled away, I glanced back at the two old men, still bickering. They didn't seem to notice I'd left.

Since I was already in Medford, I decided to give my Sadie's Farm search another try. I found a parking spot near the Medford Branch of Jackson County Library Services. The long name seemed a bit self-important, but the modern, block-long building was impressive enough to pull it off.

I went straight to the reference section and told the forty-something librarian what I was looking for. She showed me where I could find microfiche copies of old local newspapers.

"Too bad you didn't come by last week," she said. "Our official historian left on vacation a few days ago. If there were any communes around here back in 1970, he'd know about it."

Just my luck. I navigated through the archives for over two hours, but I found nothing from the Seventies that mentioned Sadie's Farm. I even checked the police log sections on the chance the cops were making regular raids on local communes, as the old guys "seemed" to remember. Got nothing.

After a couple of hours of sheet after sheet of microfiche flying past on the view screen, I was dizzy, could barely focus. I quit when I felt a headache coming on. Besides, I'd spent too damn much time on the Sadie's Farm dead end already. Sure, it might have proved helpful to know if the place had existed, but it was far from the most important part of the mystery I hoped to solve. I thought about digging through old land-ownership records, but I wasn't sure it would be worth the effort. And I'd probably go blind trying to find out if it was.

The librarian smiled at me as I passed her desk on the way out. "Any luck?"

"Afraid not, but thanks anyway."

"If you're interested, we can have anything from the historical archives at the University of Washington faxed to us. They might have something. It doesn't cost much to have copies made. I mean it's not expensive if the information is important enough to you."

"That's okay. I'm heading up to the Seattle area. Maybe I'll check at the U of W when I get there."

♦ ♦ ♦

154

According to Dad's manuscript, Braden Delaney traveled from Sadie's Farm to Port Orford on the Oregon coast. That's where Delaney met Lobo and escaped the country aboard the *Swordfish*. When I left home, I hadn't planned to visit Port Orford. But now it seemed like a worthwhile endeavor. I might at least find out if anyone remembered the *Swordfish* or something similar. "Lobo" was no doubt an alias, and a smart smuggler would change the name of his boat often.

Hell, I was already in Oregon. Port Orford was three and a half hours from Medford. Closer than Seattle. It was already almost four, and Port Orford would be as good a place as any to spend the night.

I pulled into the first gas station I came to on my way out of town. I'd only taken two steps toward the pumps when a young guy in a blue jacket and matching cap sped toward me.

"What can I get for you, sir?"

"I'm just going to fill up and get back on the road." I reached for the pump.

He adjusted his blue baseball cap, gave me a crooked grin. "First time in Oregon, sir?"

"Well, yeah. But what does that have to—"

"I'll take care of it for you." He reached past me and took the hose from the pump. "We don't have self-service at gas stations in Oregon."

"Oh?" I stepped out of the way, watched him fill the tank, clean the windows, and take my credit card inside to ring me up. Okay, all gas stations in Oregon are full-service. The only thing I've learned on this trip so far.

155

Chapter 20

I headed west to the coast, then up Highway 101, arriving in Port Orford at 7:30. The sun hadn't yet disappeared into the ocean. To my surprise, the scenic coastal highway also served as the town's main street. Good thing I slowed down, or I might have missed it.

Port Orford's most prevalent landmark was a huge concrete dock. I had to navigate down a steep road to get to it, a task made all the more difficult by the glare of the sun off the water.

I was no expert when it came to commercial fishing, but the dock was *not* what I expected. Giant cranes lifted fishing boats from the water up to the dock and lowered them onto dollies, where a pickup truck pulled them into special parking spaces. I'd never seen anything like it. If this was the way the fishing boats were handled back in the Seventies, no way Lobo could have made his arrivals and departures in secret. Another bit of evidence that Dad's story was indeed a piece of fiction. That said, if a boat called the *Swordfish* ever existed, the fishing dock was the most likely place to find someone who might have heard of it forty years ago.

I parked off to the side, away from the boats, and scanned the area for someone old enough to have been around in the early Seventies, but nearly all the dockworkers and fishermen I saw were much too young. I counted over thirty boats on the dock, and based on the remaining space, I guessed most were already in by this time of day.

Down the dock near the cranes, I noticed Salty's Dock Diner, a ramshackle restaurant that claimed to feature gifts, fishing tackle, and a museum. The sign by the door said "Breakfast/Lunch/Dinner," with "Breakfast" crossed out with a black felt pen.

Its location meant Salty's would be an easy place for local fishermen to grab a quick bite or a beer after a hard day on the water. Besides, I realized I was hungry for seafood; probably it was the ocean air. If Salty's turned out to be just as trashy on the inside, I could always bail and find a place less likely to offer salmonella as an unlisted menu item.

But instead of the smell of stale grease I'd anticipated, I was welcomed by the enticing aroma of fish on the grill and fresh-baked rolls. The interior was bright and immaculate, with clean blue-and-white-checked tablecloths on all eight tables. Each occupied by locals who all seemed to know each other. Might mean the food here was pretty good.

Dad would have loved this place. I could hear him reciting one of his mantas to me once again, "Appearances can be deceiving." An ice-cold shiver slid down my spine. I steadied myself against a display case filled with antique fishing implements. No, damn it. That tired old adage did *not* apply to Dad. It couldn't.

When a table freed up, I grabbed it and ordered fish and chips, Salty's specialty according to the waiter. Turned out to be the best I'd ever eaten. No wonder. The fish couldn't have been any fresher unless it was served swimming in a bowl of seawater. I savored every bite.

While I ate, I scouted the room for anyone old enough to have heard of Lobo or the *Swordfish*. According to Dad's story, the guy was a shady character. I figured if Lobo ever existed, a local fisherman might have known about him. A few tables away sat a couple of ancient mariners. One of them laid a few bills on the table. When they rose to leave, the other pulled a black watch cap down over his unruly shock of white hair.

I signaled the waiter, paid my check, and charged outside to catch up with the old guys.

They'd separated. I spotted one getting into a car farther down the dock. Watch Cap shuffled toward a faded green pickup.

I moved as quickly as I could, without looking like I was about to attack, and reached the truck just as the old guy grabbed the door handle. "Excuse me, sir?"

Watch Cap swung around and looked me over. He didn't say anything.

"I'm sorry to bother you, but were you by any chance around Port Orford in the early Seventies?"

He narrowed his eyes. "Who wants to know?"

"My name is Nick Castle." I extended my hand.

The old man shook it. "Charley Magruder. Mind telling me why you're so interested in my whereabouts way back then?"

I had to think fast. "Well, umm … I'm a *writer*. And I'm working on a novel. Part of it takes place here in Port Orford back in 1970." I wasn't sure where the novel-writing ruse came from, but I supposed it could turn out to be true. Someday. Good enough cover, though.

"Any money in it?"

I winced. "No, sorry."

Magruder took out a cigarette and lit it, never taking his eyes off of me. "Well, son, you might could loosen my tongue with a couple a beers."

"That I can do." I turned back toward Salty's.

He stopped me with a hand on my shoulder, tilted his head toward a nondescript cinder-block building at the top of the hill. "The Sea Dog's just up Dock Road there. Not so crowded." He winked at me. "Damn near impossible to miss, but you can follow me if you're afraid of gettin' lost."

I chuckled. "Think I can find it all right. Meet you there."

I parked my Prius in the Sea Dog lot near Magruder's pickup and followed him through the front door. He exchanged hearty greetings with everyone we passed. The Sea Dog immediately struck me as the Port Orford version of Cheers— a place where everybody knows your name. Magruder held up two fingers to the barmaid and headed straight for a particular booth in the back like a homing pigeon.

As I followed him, I looked around to get a feel for the place. The décor featured stains and gouges on the wooden tables and chairs and rips in the plastic upholstery of the booths; the walls were decorated mostly with faded photos of fishing boats and beaming guys in rain bib pants hoisting one kind of huge fish or another. I'd bet nothing new had been done to the

159

interior of the place in twenty years. Guess that amounted to atmosphere.

I nodded to Magruder. "I like this place."

"Ah, she ain't nothin' fancy. But to us old-timers, she's kinda like home … only with more people in it. It gets a bit wild at night when the band starts up. I try to be home in bed by then."

The barmaid set a brim-full mug of beer in front of each of us. Magruder sucked down about half of his in one swallow. "But the beer's cold and this place is famous for its cheeseburgers." He licked the foam from his upper lip. "You hungry?"

"Nah, I'm good." Was he hinting for me to buy him dinner? "What about you?"

Magruder shrugged. "Had me a big bowl of chowder at Salty's. Besides, cheeseburgers don't agree with my gut no more. Guess I'm gettin' too old for 'em." He sighed and stared down at his hands gripping the mug. "Getting' too damn old for most everything."

"So, how long have you been fishing here in Port Orford?"

"Did it for almost sixty years. I's only fourteen when I first started goin' out on the boats. Just a young pup, like you." Magruder studied his beer mug. "Don't get out on the water much anymore though. My son and grandson are workin' the boat these days. Miss it though." He finished off his beer. "This retirement crap is for the birds."

I nodded as if I understood. "Any chance you remember a boat called the *Swordfish* … from back in the Seventies?"

"You mean the *Silverfish*"?

160

I cocked my head to the side. "I thought a silverfish was an insect?"

Magruder laughed. "Just an ol' fisherman's joke, son." He signaled for another round.

I took a swallow of my beer. Bad idea to try to keep up with *this* old guy. "So how about the *Swordfish*? Ever heard of it?"

"Lemme see. You know? I kinda do remember a boat that might have been called somethin' like that. It wouldn't a been one of the regular fleets of fishin' boats here, though." The barmaid returned with two fresh mugs and set one in front of my almost full first beer. Magruder took the other one from her hand and winked at her. He turned back to me. "If this particular boat you're askin' about was the one I'm thinkin' it was ... um, I kinda recollect it didn't fish the same areas we did. It left port for a long spell instead of comin' back home each day like the rest of us."

I stared into my beer, waiting for my heart to stop assaulting my rib cage. I took a slow deep breath. Relax. This didn't prove anything. I finished off my first mug and pulled the second one closer.

"She always came back to Port Orford sooner or later though. Had the feelin' she didn't do much fishin'. Know what I mean?" He gave me a wink, killed another half a mug, and wiped his sleeve across his mouth.

I nodded, took another swallow. "But it would have been impossible to sneak in or out of port, right? I mean the cranes don't work in the *dark*, do they?"

"Nope, not usually. But there wasn't no cranes way back in the time you're askin' about."

161

Wait a minute. I had just witnessed the operation on the dock. Wouldn't be any way to get the boats up onto it without the cranes. Was Magruder just stringing me along for the free beer? I studied the old man more closely. Hefty gut, bloodshot eyes, bloated face, and his cheeks and nose were a road map of red veins and blotches. Classic signs of an alcoholic.

"Well, if there weren't any cranes back then, how did they get the boats on and off the dock?"

A smile tugged at the corner of his mouth. "Wasn't no big ol' cement dock back then neither. Just a pier. Wasn't nobody checkin' to see who was comin' or goin' … or when they was doin' it."

I grimaced. So much for catching him in a lie.

"If I'm rememberin' right, the captain was a strange duck. Don't recollect him that well though. Kinda stayed to hisself. But …." Magruder's eyes clouded over as if he were recalling details. Maybe just searching for his lost train of thought.

"You remember this strange duck's name?"

"Dunno if I ever heard the guy's name. Didn't care to find out. I figured whatever he was up to was kinda shady."

"Why did you think that?"

"Well, I can't say for sure if it was the boat you're inquirin' about, but the one I'm kinda rememberin' eventually got herself nabbed by the Coast Guard."

"She must have been up to something illegal, then. But do you think he was captured sometime in the Seventies?"

"Coulda been. Or maybe the Eighties. Son, I ain't sure anymore what the hell happened to *me* that far back." He chuckled. "Ain't all that clear on last week even." He shrugged. "But I guess it coulda been around then."

Two more beers arrived. I hadn't even seen Magruder order them. Maybe the barmaid just kept an eye on his beer mug and fetched another one when she saw him closing in on the bottom. She took my empties with her. When did I finish the second one?

Anyway, if Magruder's memory of the Coast Guard confiscating a boat was right, I supposed there might be an outside chance it was the *Swordfish*. Dad's story made it clear Lobo was smuggling drugs. It made sense that—if he was real—sooner or later he'd get caught. Maybe I didn't have to go any farther than Port Orford to discover there was no *Swordfish* and Lobo never existed. Then again, it's supposed to be impossible to prove a negative, except in math.

I glanced over at Magruder. "So, is there a Coast Guard station near here?"

"Yep, right down in the cove." He made a vague gesture that indicated the cove was somewhere to the south of the Sea Dog. "Can't miss it."

"Great, maybe I'll check with them. I suppose they could have some records that will tell me what I'm looking for."

"You surely could check with 'em … 'cept for one thing." His smile told me there was a punchline coming.

I played along. "What's that?"

Magruder chuckled. "Ain't a workin' Coast Guard station no more. Battened down the hatches on that sucker *a long* time ago. Been a museum goin' on ten years or more."

I tried a smile, couldn't pull it off. I wasn't sure if what I felt was frustration or relief.

163

Magruder began waxing nostalgic for the good ol' days when being a fisherman meant somethin', back when fishing offered plenty of excitement and a hell of a lot more danger. True or not, his tales would have been more interesting if I'd understood half the nautical terms he peppered them with.

Just to be polite, I stayed for a few more rounds before finally settling up with the barmaid, including one more for Magruder. I thanked the old man and said goodnight. I'd lost track of how many beers I'd had, but—since I was still ambulatory—I was pretty sure I hadn't matched Magruder. As soon as I stepped outside, the cool sea breeze slapped me across the face like a jilted ex-girlfriend. My rubbery legs threatened to drop me where I stood. Too many beers in too short a time will do that. A lesson I'd learned the hard way in college.

Probably turn out to be just another waste of time, but since I was here, I made a mental note to check with the local police, see if I could find any mention of Lobo or the *Swordfish* in their archives. If those records existed, and the authorities had stepped in, the police could have information about it *somewhere* in their files.

But now wasn't the time to be going to a police station. No. What I needed the most right now was a clean, inexpensive room, and a good night's sleep. I'd noticed the Sea Breeze Motel on the way up from the dock to the tavern. It was only a couple of blocks away.

I started to back out of my parking spot and immediately slammed on my brakes to avoid a neon-red van. I twisted around for a better look. Painted on the van's side panel was a grinning Jolly Roger with "The Prairie Pirates" on its headband and two guitars crossed like bones below. The van couldn't have been much flashier, but I hadn't even noticed it pull into the lot. I was drunker than I thought. I took a minute to regain my composure and watch the band unload its gear.

Somehow, I made it to the Sea Breeze without incident. It turned out to be a pleasant enough choice. No trouble getting a room; there couldn't have been more than four people in the whole place.

I'd check with the police tomorrow. I needed a change of pace. Based on my experience so far, I might end up spending most of my time trying to make sense out of the vague memories of old farts. And so far I'd gotten nothing but highly questionable maybes.

Chapter 21

Saturday morning, I had bacon, eggs, and grease at the First Mate Café. The coffee wasn't bad, though. Good and strong. Had three cups. Despite a hangover headache, my brain seemed to be working again. I could have slept in even more, but I wanted to get back on the road north. One more stop and I'd be out of here. Port Orford was interesting in its way, but my real destination was Carlyle University in Washington.

Turned out, the Port Orford Police Station took up half the first floor of the City Hall building. I walked through the front door at 8:30 a.m. The heavy-set, bleached-blonde woman at the front desk looked to be mid-forties. The small plaque on her desk identified her as Sylvia Pellegrini. She didn't acknowledge my arrival.

When she eventually looked up, I gave her my best smile. "Good morning, Ms. Pellegrini. My name is Nick Castle."

"It's *Officer* Pellegrini." She pointed to the name tag on her shirt.

I cringed. This was going to be fun. "Oh, right. I'm so sorry … I meant no dis—"

She held up her hand like a crossing guard. "What can the police do for you this morning, Mr. Castle?"

"I was hoping to find out if you might have a record of a criminal called 'Lobo' in your computer archives. It would have been back in the early Seventies."

Officer Pellegrini shook her head. "Can't help you there. Our computerized records only go back as far as 1995. We're a small department, three full-time officers and a few reserves and volunteers." She rolled her eyes. "As you might suspect, updating our historical records isn't much of a priority."

"I understand." I shrugged. "Sorry to have bothered you. I figured it was worth a try. Thanks anyway." I pivoted toward the door.

"Okay, now I'm curious, Mr. Castle. Why in the world would you care about someone who went by the alias 'Lobo'? I assume it *is* an alias."

"Oh, I'm sure it is … Officer. Well, umm … I'm working on a novel." I might as well embrace the ruse. "Some of it happens here in Port Orford in the Seventies."

She gave me a heavy sigh. I read disappointment.

"Well, there might be some scenes later on in the book that would take place in the Port Orford of today."

"Really? We'd … I mean Port Orford would be in your book?"

"Maybe." I nodded. "I'm thinking of including a character who's based on this Lobo guy." The more I mentioned the alleged novel-in-progress, the more embellished it became.

"So, your character would be based on someone in Port Orford you think was *real*?"

"Yeah, that's the idea."

167

"I thought novels were all make-believe."

"Yes, they're fiction, but we try to create characters who seem as real as possible." Jesus, what was I, the official spokesman for working novelists?

She leaned forward in her chair. "What makes you think this *Lobo* was ever here?"

"I saw a reference to him in an old ... diary. Written by someone who claimed to have been here in 1970."

Officer Pellegrini stared off into space. "Just think ... a novel about our very own town. Wouldn't that be something?"

"Well, it's not really ...." I decided to leave well enough alone. I was already up to my ankles in bullshit.

Officer Pellegrini peered back at me, a hint of a smile forming at the corners of her glossy pink lips. "You know what? Maybe Sophie could help you go through our old files. She's one of our volunteers. She'll be here in just a little while, if you don't mind waiting half an hour, maybe less."

"Hmm, you know maybe I will wait." Once this volunteer showed up I could make a token search and be on the road by, I checked my watch, by ten.

Of course, what I was hoping for was to find nothing at all in the records that would imply Lobo ever existed. But, even if I found out he did, I wasn't sure what that would tell me. Dad could have read about the guy somewhere. Or simply made up the character from his imagination. *Or* he could have met him in person ... if Dad was really Braden Delaney. Assuming Delaney was any more real than Lobo. Okay, enough.

♦ ♦ ♦

Twenty minutes later, Sophie Cole stepped through the front door. About my age, deep blue eyes, brunette hair pulled back in a ponytail, and a warm smile that took in the entire room, even though it felt like she aimed that smile at me. Her police volunteer uniform was obviously made with someone larger in mind.

Officer Pellegrini introduced us and gave Sophie a quick rundown of the situation, ending with, "Nick here is going to make Port Orford famous."

Sophie looked at me, then back at Pellegrini. "We're already famous."

"No, I mean famous for something more than being the westernmost point in the continental United States. This could really pump up the tourist trade."

I stood, stayed silent. Best not to curb Officer Pellegrini's misguided enthusiasm. Especially since I was her misguider.

Sophie pivoted around to me, raised an eyebrow. "Well, you don't look much like Ol' Papa Hemingway." Had she seen through my ruse already?

I grinned. "Give me a few more years at it, and you might start to see a resemblance."

"So, what's your novel called?"

"Don't have a title yet." I rubbed the back of my neck, looked down. "It's still very much in the research stage."

When I lifted my gaze back to her, she hit me with the most disarming smile I'd ever seen. "Sure, I'd be glad to help you look through those dusty old records. Emphasis on dust. But don't get your hopes up. Coming up with something that obscure is going to be as tough as finding an honest fisherman."

Magruder came to mind. "I understand, Ms. Cole. I just thought, since I'm here, I might get lucky."

She laughed.

I felt my cheeks flush. "Oh no! I didn't mean 'get lucky' in the sense of … I would never—"

She waved away my fast-crumbling apology and grinned. "It just struck me as funny, Mr. Castle." She paused. "Listen, before it gets any more awkward, how about I call you Nick and you call me Sophie."

"Deal."

We shook on it.

I followed her down the hall into the storage room, a glorified janitor's closet. No windows, so Sophie left the door open. Ancient metal filing cabinets lined one wall; a metal folding table—same army green as the cabinets—was pushed up against the opposite wall. Precarious stacks of cardboard boxes occupied the far end—an avalanche waiting to happen. This looked like it was going to be a hell of a lot more work than it was worth.

It was. We spent more than two hours of head-down focus on the reports in the archives, and we'd turned up nothing even interesting, much less any reference to this alleged Lobo character. My back hurt, my neck was stiff, and the words on the documents were starting to blur. I guessed Sophie was suffering similar afflictions.

I sank back in my chair, let go a loud sigh. "Maybe we ought to just forget the whole thing. I've taken up enough of your time already."

Sophie kept reading intently. Did she even hear me? "What are you finding?" I asked.

Still no response.

I checked my watch. Almost eleven. "You know? This Lobo guy probably never really existed." Relief flowed over me like a gentle wave.

She raised her eyes from the document, half-smiled, and handed me the file. "O ye of little faith. Take a look."

I read that a Samuel "Shark" Preston had been questioned in 1976 regarding the alleged smuggling of cocaine into the U.S. The local police couldn't get him to admit to anything, and Preston had been handed over to the DEA for further interrogation. I scanned Preston's long list of aliases. Halfway down I saw one that stopped me cold: Richard "Lobo" Hastings.

I slumped back in my chair, blindsided by a semi. Shut my eyes tight against a wave of dizziness.

"You okay, Nick? You look a little pale." Sophie rested her hand on my shoulder.

I liked the warm, gentle feel of her touch. I made a feeble attempt to wave off her concern, while I waited for the room to stop spinning. "It's nothing."

She narrowed her eyes at me. "If I had to guess, I'd say this fictional character," air quotes, "means a lot more to you than you're letting on."

"Not really. I mean, in my research, I found a reference to a guy named Lobo who ran a boat out of here back in the Seventies. I just wanted to find out if he actually existed. Just basic background stuff, ya know?"

It could still be a coincidence that Dad arbitrarily gave a fishing boat captain, running a smuggling operation out of Port Orford, the same name as a real fishing boat captain, smuggling cocaine into the county through the same port. Okay, not a coincidence. So, at least that part of the story was loosely based on fact. But that didn't mean *all* of it was true. Did it?

Sophie drew me back to the moment. "You *sure* you're all right? Can I get you some water or something?"

"What? Oh yeah, I'm fine. Didn't expect we'd ever find anything on Lobo is all."

"Well, today's your lucky day. Sometimes perseverance pays off." She spread her arms wide, flicked her wrists toward the piles of folders scattered around the table. "But this was enough to test anyone's staying power." She picked up the file she'd just showed me. "I'll make you a copy of this. Be right back."

She returned with the copy, handed it to me.

I stuffed it into my messenger bag. "Thanks."

Sophie began to pick up discarded folders and return them to their original boxes.

I grabbed some, followed her lead. "I really do appreciate you helping me with this. I don't know how I can repay you. Um, can I at least buy you lunch or coffee?"

"Aw, that's sweet of you … but I have to finish my shift." She glanced through the door at Officer Pellegrini, then turned back to me. "So, how long are you in town? I mean I suppose you could always show your appreciation by taking a girl out to dinner."

"Dinner? Oh. Sure. Of course, that's the *least* I can do. Pick somewhere nice." So much for getting back on the road. The thing was, I wasn't so anxious to barrel headlong to Sinclair, Washington, and Carlyle University.

"I know just the place. I'll take care of the reservations." She tore off a piece of paper from a scratch pad, wrote down directions to her house. "How about you pick me up around seven?"

"Perfect."

My gut told me that taking a break from my quest was a good idea. I wasn't sure just what I'd gotten myself into with Sophie Cole. Likely nothing. Hell, we'd just met. Sure, she was attractive, and I liked her. But mostly what I needed right now was some time to prepare emotionally for whatever I'd have to face up north. My search for the truth had just shifted to proving Dad *wasn't* who I'd always thought he was. But I still needed to know that truth. Fuck.

Chapter 22

I was counting on Sophie to drag me out of my emotional quagmire, or at least distract me for a couple of hours. I was nervous though. I hadn't been on a real "first date" since college. I'd known Chelsea Rutledge since we were kids at Shoat Valley Elementary.

Turned out, Sophie lived in a restored two-story Victorian on the outskirts of town. Its gingerbread trim was painted in the same bright, contrasting colors I'd seen on the famous Painted Ladies of San Francisco. The wood sign in front of the house read Cole Fine Arts Studio. The lights were off downstairs, but from what I could see in the waning sunlight, the whole bottom floor seemed to be a working painter's studio. I could just make out several large canvases mounted along the walls, and a few more on easels. Abstracts. Honestly? I couldn't tell if they were finished or not.

I followed Sophie's written instructions and climbed the stairs at the rear of the house. When she greeted me at the door of her apartment, my first thought was: *Is this the same girl I spent most of the morning with?* But what I told her was, "Wow! You look amazing."

Her smile made it clear I'd said the right thing. If Sophie had hoped to show me she was a knockout, I got the message. Her thick brunette hair, no longer stretched back in the ponytail, spilled down in waves just beyond her shoulders. She wore designer jeans and a white silk shirt, both of which made it clear that the baggy volunteer police uniform she'd worn this morning didn't do her justice. She was taller, too, which I quickly attributed to the spike heels on her black leather boots. Sophie Cole was both stylish and sexy. I was a big fan of that look. And she seemed to have turned up the dial to "ten" just for me. Really?

I, on the other hand, wore clean Levi's, my best plaid shirt, and my favorite suede jacket—the one that didn't show too many stains or smudges. Downright shabby by comparison. Of course, I'd learned long ago that no man could compete with a woman who was determined to look alluring. Why would you even want to?

Sophie had made reservations at Flatfish, an elegant restaurant with great panoramic views of the ocean. "This place is fairly expensive, so we're gonna go Dutch," she told me, punctuating her demand with a broad smile. "That way nobody feels any obligation."

"Nope, this is my treat." I held up my hands. "It's dinner. I don't have any expectations except sharing a pleasant meal with you."

We arrived a little early, so the maître d' suggested we have a drink in the bar while we waited for our window table. Over margaritas, I learned that Sophie was twenty-six, a couple of years older than me and that she'd graduated from the University of Oregon with a degree in psychology.

175

"I love psychology," she told me. "But if I ever hope to do anything with it, I'll have to go back to graduate school. I might someday … when the time is right." She glanced around the bar. "Of course, Port Orford isn't the best place to earn a ton of money, even if you own a fishing boat."

"Must be hard to make enough to live on." Jesus, that was lame.

Sophie didn't seem to notice. "Could be worse. Mom doesn't charge me rent for my apartment above her studio. I volunteer at the police department, but I earn enough to get by working a few days a week down at the Coast Guard museum … and occasionally schlepping drinks at the Sea Dog." Big grin. "Let's just say I don't have a particularly opulent lifestyle."

I smiled back. "A museum, huh. I *heard* it wasn't an active Coast Guard station anymore."

"You did?"

"Yeah, from Magruder, an old guy I met on the dock."

She raised an eyebrow. "Oh, I know Magruder. Let me guess, he was full of information until you stopped buying him beers."

I shrugged. "Something like that. He seemed to have a vague memory about a fishing boat called the Swordfish. Might have been run by this Lobo guy."

She shook her head. "I wouldn't put much stock in anything he's told you. Remember, he's an old fisherman. I doubt he's ever told the whole truth about anything in his life."

I winced, then smiled. "Yeah, that's what I figured."

"Anyway, the closest I ever come to using my psychology studies is volunteering at the police department."

"Trust me, I know the feeling. My degree's in English, as in that-and-four-bucks-will-get-you-a-latte. So why are you in Port Orford anyway? I'd imagine you'd have better prospects in Portland. Even in Eugene."

She took a sip and set her glass on the bar. "I grew up here. But I came back because my mom is …" She took in a breath. "Mom needs my help right now. She has cancer, and it's spreading." Sophie paused and looked away for a few seconds before turning back to me. "I wanted to be here for her. She doesn't agree it's necessary. Francesca Cole's the most independent woman you'll ever meet. But I'm determined to ride this through with her." She took in a breath, let it out. "She may only have a couple of good years left."

I reached over and touched her hand. "I understand what you're going through. I lost my dad to cancer about a month ago. I miss him so much." I was determined not to get all weepy in front of Sophie. "I still have my mom and sister, but it's not the same. My dad and I were … close." I shut my eyes.

"I get it." She took my hand in hers, held it when I started to withdraw it. "I never knew my dad, but my mom and I are like sisters. She's the coolest person I know." Sophie smiled.

"So, you were born here?"

"Nope. I was a toddler when Mom and I moved here in the late Eighties. Port Orford was a thriving artists' community then."

"Oh yeah. I came across a reference to that in my … research," I said.

"She's really good, by the way. Her paintings hang in galleries all over the world, and she's pretty well set financially.

177

But I know the cancer worries her more than she'll let on." She lifted her glass, held it in front of her with both hands. "Worries me, too."

Good time to alter the mood, and with impeccable clairvoyance, the host arrived to announce our table was ready.

Not surprisingly the Flatfish menu was awash with fresh local seafood. Sophie pointed out salmon was in season, and, on her recommendation, we both chose the Grilled Steelhead. I let Sophie select the wine, and she ordered a bottle of a local white pinot noir. We clinked glasses and took a sip. I was impressed. The girl knew her wines. Hell, I thought all pinot noirs were red.

With the first bite, the grilled salmon won me over. I know, it's a cliché. But it really did melt in my mouth.

Without taking her eyes off her plate, Sophie asked, "So, Nick, what's your social life like? Girlfriend?"

I smiled. This was a woman who didn't rely on subtle innuendo. "Nope. Had my share of girlfriends in college, and … well, there's someone I've been seeing back home, but I'm not convinced it's going anywhere. How about you?"

"I'm pretty much in the same boat. With barely a thousand people within driving distance of Port Orford, it's pretty slim pickin's."

"I know what you mean. I come from Shoat Valley, in Northern California. Population's about the same."

She shrugged. "Around here, guys even close to my age barely made it through high school, and most of those who did are commercial fishermen. You're the first college graduate I've met since I came back home."

"So, you don't date at *all*?"

The corner of her mouth turned up. "Only when I need companionship so badly I'm willing to throw my standards out the window for a night."

I chuckled along with her.

"After my sophomore year, I dropped out to support a boyfriend who was in grad school. We lived together, but we weren't really in love. He took his masters with him to a job back east. And by the time I graduated, Mom had gotten sick. Anyway, now it's just me and my cat, Leonardo DiCaprio." She lifted her glass and tilted it toward me, winked. "So, I really shouldn't complain when I'm sleeping with Leo every night."

I clinked my glass with hers. "Excellent point."

We discovered we liked many of the same movies and TV programs. Both of us refused to watch any of the flood of sleazy reality television shows. We'd both read every novel by Christopher Moore and Barbara Kingsolver. We both loved music. Sophie was more into classical than me, but—because of the influence of her mom and my dad—we both liked reggae and classic rock. And she was a big fan of the blues. Just like me.

"My dad turned me on to the great blues masters like B.B. King, Muddy Waters, and Robert Johnson," I said.

Sophie chuckled. "My mom plays mostly classic rock and blues while she works. But *whatever* she happens to have on her sound system, she plays it very loud. Claims it inspires her."

I sucked in air through clenched teeth. "Gee, do you think we might have been separated at birth?"

"God, I hope not." She chuckled as she refilled our glasses.

179

We both focused on what was left of our entrees for a few minutes.

Then she set down her fork and peered over at me. "So, Nick, tell me about this novel you're working on."

I stifled a grimace, waited until the tingling that swept across my neck and cheeks settled down. I'm sure she saw me flush. Foisting the ruse on Sophie didn't feel right. I chose to waffle. "Honestly, as I said, I'm still at the research stage. I hope to get going on the writing when I get back from this road trip."

"Can you tell me *anything* about it? I mean besides the fact that some of it allegedly takes place in Port Orford … and there's a character based on a guy who sometimes called himself Lobo."

"Um … I haven't got it all worked out yet, but it's going to be about something that happened back in the Seventies, and then it follows the protagonist's life afterward… how he's forced into exile because of what happened." Might as well use the narrative I already knew.

She laughed. "I'm betting it'll turn out to be a lot more interesting than it sounds."

"Me, too."

We shared a truly decadent chocolate tart and each had a glass of port.

Sophie sank back into her chair. "I'm afraid I've had a bit too much to drink."

"You're not the *only* one."

She held up an index finger. "You know what we need? A stroll on the beach to help clear our heads."

"Great idea."

"Lookout Rock Park is only a few blocks from here."

"Let's do it." I signaled for the check.

When the waiter brought it, I snatched it away before Sophie could grab it.

"Wait. I thought were going Dutch. I'm perfectly comfortable paying my half."

"And I told *you*. This is my treat. For helping me track down Lobo. And it comes with no expectations, just like I promised."

"Yeah, I remember." She grinned. "Thank you, Nick Castle. *You* are truly a gentleman."

As soon as we reached the beach, she put her hand on my shoulder for balance and pulled off her boots. Watching her wiggle her toes in the cool sand looked like fun, so I followed suit. Nice. Even with the slight breeze off the ocean, I felt warm strolling along the water's edge with Sophie. Her fingers brushed against mine, and it seemed like the most natural thing in the world to take her hand.

We were paying so much attention to each other that neither of us noticed that the tide had moved up precariously close until a surge of water soaked our feet and our jeans up to the calves. We scrambled up higher on the beach where we'd be safe from any similar surprises.

A large piece of driftwood, where we'd left her boots and my shoes, served as a place to sit. Together, we took in the gentle, lapping waves and the bright stars. Words weren't necessary. Sophie rested her head on my shoulder. Her hair smelled like lavender and mint. It seemed perfectly natural to put my arm around her and pull her close. I wanted this moment to last. Maybe I'd be able to work up the nerve to kiss her.

"I wish we could stay here like this all night." She shivered against me.

I took off my jacket and slipped it over her shoulders. "Me, too. But I guess we should go before it gets any colder."

Sophie sighed. "Yeah, you're right."

I grabbed my shoes and Sophie's boots, and we made our way barefoot back to the car.

Chapter 23

With Sophie's hand in mine, we strolled toward the stairs to her apartment at the back of the house. On the way, we passed the two huge picture windows of the now brightly lit ground-floor studio.

She gestured toward the thin, attractive older woman in paint-splattered white overalls. "Well, there she is, my mom … the famous Francesca Cole. Still working like crazy. I think she's trying to produce as much as she can in the time she …" Sophie took a moment to compose herself. "Mom would never admit it, though. She'd claim it was just another fit of inspiration."

I watched Francesca add streaks of yellow with bold, slashing strokes to the canvas in front of her. Her hair, dark like Sophie's, but with exotic streaks of gray, fell down her back in a French braid that whipped back and forth when she moved. I guessed she was mid-fifties. Even outside we could hear the strains of "Proud Mary" pumping through the studio's sound system. Francesca belted out the lyrics right along with Tina Turner. She stepped back to assess her work and reached over to pick up a glass of wine. That's when she noticed us. I expected her to be embarrassed after being caught with her guard down, but she smiled and waved at us, without a hint of self-consciousness.

We both returned Francesca's wave. She studied me for a few seconds, gave Sophie a sly thumbs-up grin, and punched in another song on her disc player—sounded like "Magic Man." She spun back around to the huge easel and immediately burst into song again in that uninhibited way most people do only when they think they're alone.

Sophie squeezed my arm. "I'd introduce you, but I don't like to take her away from a painting when she's that engrossed. She'd have invited us in if she was ready to take a break."

I nodded toward the impressive two-story Victorian. "This is a nice place."

"A few years ago, she had the place remodeled, so now it's basically a huge studio with two separate apartments up top. We each have our own space—kitchen, laundry, everything— and I'm near enough to step in if she falls again … or has to go to the hospital. Even though she isn't happy about it, she allows me to keep track of her with a baby monitor. I call it a 'mommy monitor,' but she still hates it."

I turned back to Sophie. "Seems like a damn good idea."

She smiled and snaked her arm through mine, and we headed to the stairs. "How 'bout a nightcap?" She grimaced. "Christ. Just slap me if I ever use another worn-out cliché. The thing is, I just don't want this evening to be over yet."

"Me either. I've never met anyone quite like you, Sophie Cole."

She laughed, and we climbed the stairs with our arms entwined.

184

Once inside, Sophie shed the jacket I'd lent her and laid it over a chair. The pounding beat of "Magic Man" had died down. Sophie pointed at the floor. "Mom's being courteous. Guess she wants us to be able to talk without shouting." She tilted her head toward the sound system on the shelf under the TV. "Why don't you put on some music? I'll get the drinks."

I ran my finger down her CD rack and was amazed to discover that Sophie was the only other person I knew, besides Dad, who owned Jimi Hendrix's posthumous *Blues* CD. I put it on. As soon as I sat down on the couch, a big black-and-white cat sprang up and settled in beside me. I stroked the cat's thick fur. "So, you must be Leonardo DiCaprio. I thought you'd be taller."

Sophie returned with two glasses of red wine and set them on the coffee table in front of me. "I see Leo likes you. That's a good sign; he usually shies away from strangers." She eyed the cat and shook her head in mock despair. "Oh, Leo, say it ain't so. You were always a one-person cat."

I patted the couch on the other side of me.

Sophie held up an index finger. "Be back in a sec, but I've *got* to get out of these wet jeans, and I'll see if I can find something for you." She stopped at the door to her bedroom and whirled back around. Eye roll. "Okay, just for the record, I did *not* say I wanted to slip into something more comfortable."

I grinned. "Duly noted."

She shot me a smile and vanished through the door. When she returned a few minutes later, she wore an oversized Oregon Ducks football jersey that fell to mid-thigh, her jeans in one hand and a pair of sweatpants in the other. She shrugged. "You were expecting maybe a sexy see-through negligee?"

185

"Oh, no worries. I think you're making the perfect fashion statement." In fact, at that moment, Sophie Cole was the sexiest woman I'd ever seen. I wasn't sure how she managed it.

She tossed me the sweatpants. "Fork over those wet jeans. I'll stick 'em in the dryer with mine."

I stood up, removed my belt.

"If you'd rather, you can change in the bathroom. Or I can turn my back to give you a little privacy."

"If you do, you'll miss seeing my Sponge Bob underpants," I said straight-faced, as I pulled off my jeans.

"Ah, boxer-briefs, the choice of the fashionable young hipster." She took the jeans from me.

"I try to keep current on all the important fashion trends." I pulled on the sweatpants as I watched her disappear with the wet clothes into a small room off the kitchen.

When she returned, she plopped down next to me on the couch, picked up her glass and handed mine to me. "To the most interesting evening I've had in a long, long time."

"Was for me, too." I reached over and tapped her glass with mine.

Leonardo DiCaprio yawned, stretched, and hopped off the couch.

I took a sip. Then I took a chance. I reached for her glass, set both down on the table, and pulled her into my arms. When she melted into my embrace, I kissed her.

She kissed me back, and each kiss that followed upped the passion a little more.

When we came up for air, she leaned back and brushed her hand across her forehead. "Whew, we finally got *that* over

186

with. I wanted to kiss you out there on the beach, but I didn't want to come off as too aggressive."

"You were a perfect lady the whole time," I assured her.

"Nick, I want you to know that I don't usually invite men up here. Certainly not on the first date."

"I'm not making any assumptions at all. I just really wanted to kiss you."

Sophie grinned. "Exactly the way I felt." She locked eyes with me. "You're a nice guy, Nick Castle." She ran a finger along my cheek.

When I put my arm around her and pulled her close, she rested her head on my chest. "So, I guess you'll be heading over to Portland first thing in the morning."

I hesitated. "Yeah, then on up to Washington."

"And that means we probably won't ever see each other again."

"Jesus, I hope that's not true. I'm not likely to forget *you* any time soon." I combed my fingers through her hair.

"Well, in that case, I'd be an inexcusably bad hostess if I made you go back to some cold, lonely motel room on your last night ever in Port Orford. You have to wait for your jeans to dry anyway. Why don't you stay here … you can sleep on the couch." She hopped up. "I'll get you a pillow and some blankets."

"I don't want you to go to any trouble on my account."

She rolled her eyes. "What trouble? It's just a blanket and a pillow. Besides, I'll never hear the end of it if my mom thinks you *didn't* spend the night. I have a reputation to uphold," she chuckled, "at least with her." Sophie took a step toward her bedroom door then swung back. She sucked in a breath. "All joking aside, I'm not ready for you to walk out of my life just yet."

The warm rush exploding through my body caught me by surprise. Before I could respond, she disappeared into the bedroom. With a bass drum thumping in my chest, I couldn't muster a coherent response anyway.

When Sophie reappeared in the doorway, she was carrying a couple of pillows and a comforter. She put them on the coffee table and plopped down on the couch next to me. I pulled her close. As she snuggled against me, it was as if we'd melded together into a single entity. She felt perfect in my arms.

Nestled together on the couch, we laughed, we talked. And talked. About everything and nothing. We watched *The Princess Bride* on the classic movie channel, finished off the bottle of wine, and opened another. The last time I noticed the clock on the disc player, it was 2:30 in the morning. Neither of us had even yawned.

Chapter 24

The sun was just filtering through the blinds when we awoke, still nestled together under the comforter on the couch.

Sophie snuggled against me, slowly disengaged herself from my arms. "I've never slept better in my life. You, sir, are one cozy cuddler." She stood up. "Thank you for being such a gentleman last night."

I beamed. It had been fun; just holding Sophie close felt special, felt right. I could get used to this. Something was going on here. The warmth wafting through me was a result of more than just sleep. I felt it every time I looked at Sophie. I saw it in her eyes, too.

She busied herself making coffee, then looked over at me. "Do you have time for breakfast? I make a mean cinnamon-roll waffle."

"Sounds great."

Turned out she had real Canadian maple syrup, too. We wolfed down the waffles as if we hadn't eaten in weeks. I had two. But we couldn't stall forever. She had to get ready for work, and I needed to check out of the motel and hit the road to Seattle.

We took a few selfies of us together and a few single shots of each other. Then Sophie entered my number and email address into her phone, and I did the same with hers.

We embraced one last time at the door of her apartment.

"I really like you, Nick Castle," she murmured against me. "But I understand this doesn't have to be anything more than a ... wonderful, one-time thing."

"I don't *want* you to be a one-time thing," I whispered back.

She hugged me tighter.

When she eased her grip, I released her and responded in the most sophisticated way I could muster at the moment. I studied my foot, scraped my shoe on the landing, then peered out at a stand of trees in the distance. "You know? I could swing by Port Orford on my way back to California."

"Oh, Nick, that would be wonderful." Delighted grin. "Chances are, I'll be thinking about you the whole time you're gone."

"Meeting you is the best thing that's ever happened to me, Sophie."

At that moment, all I wanted was to forget my quest to prove Dad was or wasn't Braden Delaney and just settle in here with Sophie ... for as long as whatever this was between us lasted. But I couldn't. Not now. Not when I'd discovered that some guy called "Lobo" actually existed and had spent time in Port Orford. Just as Dad's story said.

No telling what I was about to discover at Carlyle, but how could I move on with my life if I didn't uncover the truth?

We kissed one last time, and I headed down the stairs. There seemed to be a lot more steps than there were last night.

190

I glanced back up in time to return her smile and wave before she turned away and closed the door.

I missed her already.

♦ ♦ ♦

Following my GPS's lead, I headed up the coast on Highway 101 to Florence, about two hours away. From there, I'd cut over to I-5, a straight shot through Portland and up to Seattle. Along the way, I noticed a lot of empty houses and storefronts, as if people had abandoned them in a hurry. The few active art studios and occupied homes were outnumbered by truck repair and body shops. It seemed that folks around here did a lot of driving, but they didn't do it very well.

I'd planned to spend my time on the road creating a strategy for ferreting out any information about Braden Delaney—or Jim Castle—at Carlyle University. But I never got to that plan.

Sophie occupied my mind the whole way. I caught myself turning up a song on the radio because I wanted her to hear it. I mentioned aloud things I saw along the way as if she were sitting in the passenger seat. I'd dated several girls in my life, but I'd never met anyone like Sophie. I wanted … needed to get to know her better. She'd enticed emotions from me I didn't know I had. No other woman had ever done that. I didn't have a clue where my adventure to find the truth about Dad might lead, but I *did* know my return route would detour through Port Orford.

Yes, I'd have to admit to her that I lied about researching a novel. Well, in a way I was, but it was *not* my real motivation for this trip. She deserved to know the truth about me and

191

whatever I was about to find out at Carlyle. The specter of Lobo sent a chill down my spine every time it forced its way back into my consciousness.

I'd been on the road nearly five hours by the time I sailed through Portland. I stopped for a break and a burger at a Dairy Queen just across the Columbia River in Vancouver. GPS indicated it would take me four more hours to get to Seattle. By the time I arrived, it would be after six—too late to make the two-hour drive to Sinclair. I decided to spend the night in Seattle and head off in the morning.

Whatever I found out, I'd deal with it. But I had to know the truth.

Chapter 25

At 5:45 in the afternoon, Seattle area traffic was much worse than I'd ever seen. Rush hour was only a rumor back home in Shoat Valley. Lesson learned. Finally, I couldn't take any more of these commuter zombies trying to sneak through the gridlock. So, I pulled into the first place I saw with a vacancy—the Top Value Motel. It was cheap and close to the exit for I-90, my most direct route to Sinclair.

The slogan plastered on the front of the motel claimed it was "The perfect place for peaceful repose." The diction of the alliterative slogan was a hell of a lot more elevated than the motel's appearance, which featured several cracks along the walls, graffiti painted over with colors seemingly chosen at random, and a broken stairway repaired by someone more committed to speed than safety. I heard Dad's voice in my head: "You get what you pay for." But I was just too exhausted to care.

I chose the glass door without the "Use Other Door" sign and entered the lobby. Sitting in a rocking chair at the counter was an elderly woman, with an old-lady blue perm and a brown-and-pink shawl covering her shoulders. She was knitting. Only thing missing was an embroidered "Home Sweet Home" cross-stitch framed on the wall and doilies on the chair arms. Not what I expected.

She looked at me over her glasses, set her knitting aside. "Good afternoon, dear." She reached for the registration book. "Do you have a reservation?"

I held back a laugh. In this place? "No, ma'am, I'm afraid I don't."

She scanned the book, smiled at me. "No problem, dear. I see we have a vacancy." She rotated the register around to face me.

I signed in, slid it back to her.

She glanced at it. "How long will you be staying with us, Mr. Castle?"

"Um, just tonight."

"That'll be seventy-five dollars." She gave me a warm, grandmotherly smile. "We ask that our guests pay in advance. We take cash or credit cards."

I handed her my card.

"We won't send it through, of course, until you check out and all the charges have been calculated." She ran my card through the machine, handed it back to me, and pointed to the receipt so I could see that no totals were yet entered. And she did it all without ever leaving her chair. She showed me the location of room 21 on the site map, handed me the key-card. Then she took my hand in both of hers and looked me in the eye. "I'm the manager. Please contact the front desk if there's anything we can do to make your stay with us more comfortable."

How sweet. "Thank you, I will."

"I hope your stay with us is everything you hoped for."
She smiled at me, squinted.

Wait, did she just wink?

♦ ♦ ♦

I stepped into a room painted the color of regurgitated scrambled eggs. On the other hand, no insects seemed to be crawling along the walls. I took that as a good sign but resolved not to look too closely. Besides, I'd been on the road for close to nine hours, and last night Sophie and I had talked, laughed, and cuddled on the couch all night before we finally fell asleep sometime after two.

Not that I was complaining about sleep deprivation. Remembering last night with Sophie felt as if a rising sun were slowly warming me from the inside.

I shucked my T-shirt and jeans, flipped off the lights, and plopped down on the cool sheets. I was asleep in seconds.

My cell phone jarred me awake. The display told me I'd slept almost an hour and a half and the caller was my sister, Shelby.

I sat up on the edge of the bed. "Hey, Shel."

"Hello, stranger."

"So, you're back home for the summer."

"Yep. Sorry I didn't get to see you before you took off on your adventure."

"My adventure?"

She laughed. "Yeah, Mom says you're on some kind of mysterious road trip. To clear your head and take some time to think about Dad."

"Mom said all that?" I stood, began pacing.

195

"Okay, maybe not *exactly* that, but that's pretty much what she implied."

"Well, I guess that's close enough." I managed a ragged laugh. "I just needed to get away for a while, you know?"

"Yeah, I have trouble accepting that Dad is gone, too." She seemed to be trying to catch her breath.

I felt all the energy seep out of me, as I slumped back down on the edge of the bed, "God, I miss him."

"I *know*. Me too, Nick. But you and Dad always had something special. That father-and-son thing. I'm still a little jealous." Weak laugh.

"Yeah, I thought we did, too." Until Braden Delaney's story changed everything.

"You *thought* you did? Are you high, Nick? Any two people closer than you and Dad would have to be Siamese twins."

I forced a chuckle. "I know. Guess I'm just a little confused about a lot of things these days."

"Well, you'll work it all out, Nicky-Boy; you and Dad always were good at adapting."

Keyword: "were." I stared out into the dark motel room. "At the moment, I'm in Seattle. There are some things I want to check out up here."

"Seattle? Like the Space Needle? And the Rock and Roll museum ... the one with the giant guitar?"

"Yeah, something like that. Tell Mom I'm doing fine."

"Cool, I'll relay the message. Can't wait to hear all the sordid details of your travels. Oh, and Nick?"

"Hmm?"

"Eat a lot of fresh salmon up there. I hear it's good for you, and you'll never get anything like it in Shoat Valley."

"Good point." Brought me back to last night. Sitting at the table at the restaurant with Sophie enjoying each other … and the best salmon I'd ever eaten.

A tentative knock on the motel room door.

"Gotta go, Sis. Someone's at the door." Housekeeping at this hour? Wrong room? Was there a chance in hell it was Sophie?

"Okay but keep in touch so Mom won't worry. And for Christ's sake, call Chelsea. She's worried sick about you."

Gut punch. Of course, I should have called Chelsea. "Yeah, I know. I will." But things were different now.

A louder knock. Has to be housekeeping. Sophie would call first.

Chapter 26

Shouting out, "Be with you in a sec," I stepped into my jeans, pulled on my T-shirt, and shuffled to the door in my stocking feet. When I flipped the on the light switch next to the door, the room was a hell of a lot brighter than I remembered. Not necessarily a good thing.

The shattered peephole was useless. I cracked open the door just enough to see a woman in a black vinyl micro-mini and a low-cut, neon-red top. I guessed she was at least thirty, but it was tough to tell under all that makeup. She looked like an escapee from a porno cartoon. I blinked and shook my head, but the image just wouldn't go away.

"Hey there, handsome. Interested in a little company?" She leaned in as if she were afraid I hadn't noticed her cleavage.

I stared at her in stunned silence.

"It can get real lonely in a strange town, sugar … especially at night." She gave me a wink and a full-teeth smile.

I found my voice. "Thanks for the offer, but I don't think so."

"A good-lookin' guy like you … I'll give you a special rate."

"Look, lady, I don't want to be rude, but I'm not interested." I tried to push the door shut, but she moved forward just enough to block it.

"Honey, you should call me 'Chrystal,' with a 'y.' We should be on a first-name basis since we're about to become *real* close friends. You're in for the experience of your life … for only"—she looked me over— "fifty bucks."

I glanced beyond her into the darkened parking lot. One of the few working exterior lights in the lot revealed a guy in a nondescript black sedan who never took his eyes off us as he lit a cigarette. Shit.

While I was distracted, Chrystal pushed past me into the room. "Tell you what. You're so cute, I'm gonna give you a freebie."

"Please, I already told you. I don't want *anything* from you … free or otherwise."

She doffed her top with one quick move, like a magician pulling a rabbit out of a hat. Make that two rabbits. "Come on now, handsome, you know you don't want to pass up *these* babies." They couldn't possibly be real. Her gravity-defying breasts looked like overfilled water balloons about to burst. If I wasn't worried she was setting me up to be robbed or worse, I might have laughed out loud.

In one smooth motion, she unzipped and dropped her skirt. I decided my best option was to act forcefully. "I'm sorry, miss, but you'll have to leave. I told you I'm *not* interested." I tried to step around her toward the door.

She slid over in front of me. "And I told *you* to call me Chrystal, sugar." She shoved me hard enough that I stumbled backward and fell onto the bed. Before I could right myself, she

199

straddled me like a bull rider, her fingers busy with my belt buckle.

I struggled to push her off, but I couldn't get enough leverage. I didn't want to get too rough with her. She was, after all, a lady—if you were willing to stretch the definition—and Dad had taught me there was *never* a reason to hit a woman.

I grabbed her shoulders. tried to shove her away. "Damn it! Get the hell off me." I gave her my best fake tough-guy look. "I want you out of my room right *now*!"

"C'mon, Baby, stop pretendin' you aren't interested." She hopped up and yanked my jeans down to my knees. While I struggled to pull my pants back up, she tossed her tiny wisp of panties aside and flopped down on her back next to me.

"Come on, honey, it's *real* obvious you want me," she cooed, as she reached over and ran her hand over my crotch.

I gave up the struggle to get my jeans back up, rolled away from her onto my side, and tried to push myself off the bed. But Chrystal slithered over, pulled me down on top of her, and wrapped her legs around me.

I tried to get off her, but she had me in one hell of a leglock. She gyrated beneath me, screaming a frantic parody of an orgasm. "That's right, baby. Give it *all* to Chrystal hard and deep! I need it NOW!" It was as if she were auditioning for a role in a porno movie and everyone within a mile of the motel was in on the decision. Or maybe she was signaling someone outside. Damn, did I latch the door?

That's when a bearded hulk charged in. The gorilla stomped over to the bed. "Take your fuckin' hands off my wife. I'm gonna *kill* you, you son of a bitch!" He pulled me off the bed and slammed me against the wall, knocking the lamp off

200

the nightstand in the process. I was overwhelmed by a tsunami of muscles, tattoos, and sweat.

Chrystal clutched the brute's arm with one hand while pretending to try to cover her bare breasts with the other. "Please, Artie. Don't hurt him. He didn't mean nothin'. We was just havin' a little conversation." Her argument might have been more convincing if she hadn't been standing there buck-naked, her clothes strewn around the room as if they'd exploded off her.

"I've never seen her before in my life!" I wheezed, determined not to break into tears. "Honest, she just busted in here."

Chrystal tugged at the hem of his gaudy yellow Hawaiian shirt. "I'm just trying to make a little money, Baby. You know we need cash real bad."

Artie took his hands off me and turned to her. "Yeah, but this ain't the way I want my wife earnin' it."

I took the opportunity to inch my way toward the door, yanking up my pants on the way. If I escaped, I was sure they'd steal everything I had, but at least I'd be alive.

"Artie, maybe he can just, you know, make a donation or somethin'." She nodded toward me. "I promise, we didn't even do nothin'."

Just as I reached for the doorknob, Artie swung around and lunged at me. He crashed against the wall when I spun away from his grasp, the same way I'd avoided tacklers back in high school. But instead of doing a touchdown celebration dance, I was huddled against the wall shaking in fear.

Chrystal scurried over and wrapped Artie in a bear hug. "Please, Baby, I'm sure he'd be willin' to give us *somethin'*.

But only if you promise not to hurt him." She spun back to face me. "Right, Sugar? A couple hundred and we're all square. Whaddya say?" She glanced at Artie, who scowled at me like a rabid grizzly more interested in eating my head than taking my money. She tried to turn him away from me by grabbing his arm and pulling him around to face her. "A few hundred, huh, Artie? That'd be enough, wouldn't it? That way nobody hasta get hurt."

Artie shrugged, but never took his eyes off me. "I dunno. Maybe."

My sigh of relief came out more like a moan.

Chrystal slunk over close to me and whispered, "You better make it quick, handsome, before Artie changes his mind. He's got an *awful* temper." She picked up her skirt from the floor.

Before I could respond, the hulk rushed me again.

Chapter 27

The door flew open and two uniformed policemen swooped into the room, guns thrust out in front of them in the standard two-handed cop grip. "Police! Nobody move!" The biggest of the two pulled Artie off me and jammed him face-first against the same wall, while the other handcuffed him.

Chrystal bolted for the door, pulling her top over her head as she ran. She slammed right into the older of two plainclothes cops standing in the doorway. It was the same guy I'd seen smoking in the car earlier. But now he looked more like a rumpled detective than a pimp.

He shoved Chrystal toward his partner, who took her by the elbow and handed her over to one of the uniformed cops.

The older detective leaned down and lifted her panties from the floor with the barrel of his gun and flipped them to her. "Here, put your damn clothes back on, such as they are." He holstered his weapon and flashed his badge. "Detective Sergeant Spander, Seattle PD, Vice. I'm gonna need to see some ID, Mister …"

"Castle. Nick Castle." I wiped my sweaty palms on my T-shirt, managed to dislodge my driver's license from my wallet, and handed it to him.

"Just procedure." Spander glanced at it, looked me over, then gave my license back to me. He gestured to his partner. "This is Detective Chow."

Chow flashed his ID; we exchanged nods.

I shifted back to Spander. "I swear this woman just charged in here and started shucking her clothes, Detective. I tried to tell her I wasn't—"

He waved me off. "We're not here for you, Mr. Castle. We're familiar with their MO. We've been keepin' an eye on these two, and this time we were ready for 'em. Had to give 'em enough time to work the scam so we could catch 'em in the act. Sorry if you got roughed up. Are you all right? Do you need medical attention?"

"Nah, I'm fine, just a little shaken up is all." Since the cops arrived, my breathing had calmed down, but I was still a little woozy.

Now that Chrystal was dressed again, one of the uniformed cops recited her Miranda rights while he cuffed her.

Spander gestured to my undone jeans. "I suggest you finish dressing, too."

Willing my hand to stay steady, I managed to zip up and buckle my belt. "She did this … I mean I wasn't—"

"No need to explain, Mr. Castle. As I said, we know their MO."

I sucked in a deep breath, eased it back out.

"Pretty much caught 'em red-handed, but we'll need your statement." He nodded to Chow, who exited the room. "I'm guessin' you're not too anxious to come back all the way from California to testify if this ever goes to trial. Most likely they'll cop a plea. Afraid, though, we'll have to keep whatever cash or credit cards they took from you. Evidence." He took out a notepad. "If you'll just write down your address, we'll mail it to you, but it might take a while."

"It's okay, I didn't give them anything."

"Better check your wallet just to be sure, sir."

Damn it. I hadn't been able to keep an eye on Chrystal while the ape was manhandling me. I took a quick inventory, then a relieved breath. "Looks like it's all here, Detective."

"You were lucky." Spander offered me a crooked smile. "Welcome to Seattle, Mr. Castle. I apologize for the behavior of some of our less-than-upstanding citizens."

Chow returned and handed me a form. "Just need you to give us the details of what happened here as best you can remember them." He set the paper on the tiny desk near the door. "If you'd rather, you can come down to the station tomorrow and fill it out there. It's been my experience, though, that it's best to do it while the details are fresh in your mind."

"I'll do it here."

He handed me a pen.

While I was reading the form, Spander did a quick check of the room. I followed his gaze. Given the rumpled sheets and the mattress pulled partway onto the floor, the room looked a lot more like a crime scene than the advertised "perfect place for peaceful repose."

"Looks like we're done here." Spander stood by the door, nodded to the cops to escort Chrystal and Artie out. Spander stopped Chrystal at the door with a hand on her shoulder. "So, you two are right back fleecing unsuspecting out-of-towners, despite what the judge told you last time. She's not gonna be happy you've violated your parole." He smirked at

205

her. "Startin' to look like you might as well use the county lockup as your home address."

He waved them through the door. Turning back to me, he smiled. "Let me give you a little advice, son. Don't open the door for anyone you don't know."

I nodded, felt my cheeks flush. Most five-year-olds knew not to open the door to strangers. Dad had taught me better.

I completed the report, signed it, and handed it to Chow.

He touched my arm. "You sure you're all right? You look kinda pale."

"I'm okay. I just need a minute to process what happened here."

He nodded. "You probably just need a good night's sleep. Let me help you get that mattress back on the bed."

Together we wrestled the mattress into place. I glanced at the pile of sheets on the floor, shook my head. "You know? Just leave the mess. I'm getting out of this dump anyway."

He winked, nodded. "Smart move."

Chapter 28

Alone, I slumped down into the only chair in the room. I waved my hand through the air as if that might somehow diffuse the reek of Artie's sweaty body and the cheap perfume Chrystal must have bathed in.

How the hell had she known I was here? I hadn't left the room since I arrived. Wait. The desk clerk. Shit. That sweet old lady probably earned kickbacks for steering Chrystal to guys traveling alone. Jesus, how naïve could I be? Another lesson learned.

I packed up and headed to the motel office. Time to man up, to stop acting like a kid lost in the big city.

The office was empty, the little old grannie nowhere to be found. If she somehow didn't hear Chrystal faking the throes of ecstasy, she sure as hell couldn't have missed the commotion of the police raid.

"I'd like to speak to the manager," I said, loud enough to be heard no matter where she might be hiding.

A forty-something guy in a black tank top and baggy brown cargo shorts shuffled in from a back room. Three gold chains were proudly displayed outside his tank top and a silver cross dangled from his right ear. Neither he nor his outfit had been washed recently. His thinning hair was slicked back, which caused his bald spot to shine through, and his beard was so sparse it looked as if someone had thrown random patches of dark hair at his face. "Somethin' I can help you with?"

"I'd like to speak with the older lady who was here when I checked in."

"My grandma's gone for the day. I'm the night manager."

"Do you have a business card?"

He pulled his card from a desk drawer but held on to it. "Why do you want my card, sir?"

I reached over and grabbed it. "So, I'll be sure to spell your name correctly when I fill out my report at the police station in the morning." Yes, I was bluffing.

"Why would you—"

"Because I know you're the one who sent that crazed hooker and her Neanderthal sidekick to my room, and I'm sure the police will want to talk to you about it."

He forced a smile. "Wait. That's not really necessary, is it?

I looked him in the eye. "I'm surprised they haven't been to see you already."

His face turned ashen. He tried for a friendly good-ole-boy grin. Came off more like a sneer. "Look, we're all adults here. I'm sure we can come up with a compromise … without involving the cops."

I glared at him.

"What if I were to, say, refund your money? That way everybody walks away without a scratch."

I rubbed my shoulder and grimaced at the pain, let him stew for a while, then narrowed my eyes at him. "I want it in cash."

"No problem, sir." He shuffled off to the back and returned with my seventy-five bucks.

"Fine, now hand over my credit card receipt."

He flipped through a pile of receipts, found mine, and held it out. "I hope you don't think I'm running anything illegal—"

I snatched the receipt out of his hand and headed for the door.

He called after me. "So … you won't need to involve *me* in any of this, then. No harm no foul. Right?"

Without looking back, I waved his business card at him as if I were flipping him off and marched out the door.

Once I found a room in a cleaner, nicer place, I'd get something to eat. Now that the hamster wheel in my gut had slowed down, I realized I was starving.

I'd just tossed my suitcase and backpack on the bed at the Holiday Inn when Sophie texted: *Just wanted to make sure u made it to Seattle safe and sound.*

Happy butterflies flitted around in my chest. How did she manage to do that to me by merely sending me a text? Damn, I missed her.

I texted her back: *Yep, just checked in. Going to grab something to eat. Call you tonight? Around 8:00?*

Sophie: *Counting on it.*

I had no intention of telling her about being accosted by Chrystal and Artie. It was terrifying at the time; I was convinced I was going to be robbed, beaten, and left for dead. But now that it was over, what I felt most was embarrassment. I'd chalk it up to a consequence of choosing a cheap motel in a big city. Another lesson learned.

I chose to get my first-ever meal in Seattle at Denny's. I know, but it was only a block down the street from the Holiday Inn. I ordered the Lumberjack Slam breakfast—eggs, toast, hash browns, ham, sausage, and bacon—and dove in. I might have to deal with the consequences later, but I hadn't eaten anything since I picked up a burger just across the Columbia from Portland. And with all that had happened tonight, Portland felt like two days ago.

Time to tamp down the adrenaline a bit. After all, I wasn't some ravenous homeless person hoovering up the first solid meal I'd had in a week, even though that's probably the impression I was giving to the other patrons in the place. I sucked in a breath, eased it out, then approached the remnants of my meal like a human being.

I took the opportunity to flip through the files in my brain. Was my quest just one big, stupid mistake? Someone who used the alias "Lobo" had really existed. So what? Not like it's such an uncommon nickname. And it didn't suddenly make Dad's entire manuscript a memoir … didn't mean it *wasn't* either. Maybe I was on a fool's journey, continuing to chase an answer that I didn't really want to know. If I discovered Dad *wasn't* the person I'd worked so hard to emulate my whole life, what was he? What did that make me?

All this speculation made my head spin. But if I gave up now, I'd never know the truth. And, admit it, not knowing would haunt me forever. I glanced down at my plate. Nothing left but streaks of egg yolk and tiny rivulets of grease.

♦   ♦   ♦

I was moving a little slowly in the morning. Last night's wrestling match with Artie had left me stiff and sore. But it hardly mattered now. Not after I'd been on the phone with Sophie until after midnight. I couldn't remember when it had been so easy to talk with someone. Once again, Sophie was the highlight of my day. I sensed a pattern.

It was Seattle, so there was a Starbucks a block from the motel. I ordered a warmed-up breakfast sandwich and a double cappuccino. Okay, but I made them better at Book Castle. By the time I'd filled the gas tank, it was after ten.

An hour out of Seattle proper, traffic started to thin. Even so, it was almost one o'clock when I pulled onto the Carlyle University campus and found a visitor's spot near the student union. While I fed the meter, I took the opportunity to check out the campus. I just wanted to get a feel for the place.

Yes, I was stalling. My heart was thumping at the site where Dad's novel started. This was the place where I'd find out if the bombing of the ROTC building really happened back in 1970, and if someone named Braden Delaney set it off. If all that turned out to be what happened, I'd be one step closer to the truth. A truth I wasn't yet ready to face.

On the other hand, if there was no evidence that anything exploded on campus and no record of a student by that name,

I'd be able to let go of my obsession that Jim Castle and Braden Delaney were one and the same. I hoped.

Chapter 29

The Carlyle campus featured tall evergreens and immaculate grounds. A cursory look around told me that most buildings had been constructed long ago, although the sprawling glass-and-metal design of the student union shouted brand new. In late May the campus was almost deserted. The regular students had likely fled after spring term and summer classes must not have begun yet. My timing could have been a lot better.

I headed for the oldest building I could see. Figured it was most likely the library. Good guess. The plaque over the high-arched entrance to the Crawford Memorial Library read "Erected 1935." A good place to start my research. If any place had information about a campus event that happened over four decades ago, the university library would be it. They'd likely have local newspaper accounts, possibly going all the way back to the time the school was established.

According to the directory in the library lobby, the archives were one floor down. I took the stairs.

I wasn't sure what I expected to find, but it wasn't the complete shambles that spread out before me. Computers on the ground, unconnected cables were everywhere. I nodded a greeting to an attractive, dark-haired woman in designer jeans and a Carlyle Coyotes T-shirt. I guessed mid-forties.

"I'm looking for the historical archives," I said.

She stepped gingerly through the debris toward me and offered a sympathetic smile. "This is the right place, just not the right time." She nodded to the chaos behind her. "We're taking advantage of the interterm break to upgrade our computers. We're probably the last place on campus not using the cloud." She shrugged. "We should have been the first, but ... *politics*."

My shoulders slumped.

"I'm Samantha Mondale, the reference librarian for the archives." She held out her hand.

I shook it. "Nick Castle."

"Sorry, Mr. Castle, we can't access any of the computers at the moment. But maybe there's still something I can do for you. What are you looking for?"

"I'm interested in confirming an event that supposedly happened on campus in the spring of 1970."

"What kind of event?

"A bombing ... of the ROTC building during the student protests."

She looked at me wide-eyed. "Wow! Something like that, we'd at least have newspaper accounts. If you're a grad student, I can try to find them for you."

"I'm not a student."

She winced. "That makes it a little tricky. You'll need a visitor's pass. That'll only allow you to use the computers, but you'd be able to access the whole library here digitally." She gestured to the chaos behind her. "Sorry. As you can see that's not going to happen today."

"So, what about the papers themselves? Don't you have an archive of them?"

"Of course, but access to documents that old is restricted to faculty and authorized graduate students. For research purposes." Clenched half-smile. "There's often only one copy of the older pieces in the archive."

What the hell, were the gods against me? "Guess I'm outta luck." A disappointed sigh escaped before I could stop it.

"If you leave your name and number, I'd be happy to call you when the computers are available again."

I twisted back around to see her set a notepad on the counter.

"We should be up and running sometime next week. We need to get all this done before the Memorial Day weekend."

"I'm not sure I'll still be around then. But who knows?" I wrote my name and cell number on the pad and slid it back to her.

She glanced down at the pad, offered a friendly smile. "I'm sorry I couldn't be more helpful, Mr. Castle."

"I understand." Actually, what I understood was I should have looked at a damn calendar before I made the trip up here. Lessons learned just kept on coming. Maybe I should start writing these down.

♦ ♦ ♦

I headed toward the extensive athletic facilities—Dad's story said the ROTC building had been near the football field. It was, but the ROTC facility I found was a large, two-story brick building, weathered all right, but it didn't look old enough to

215

have been around in 1970. Made sense. If I were replacing a building that had burned to the ground, I'd choose brick, too.

When I walked through the front door of the ROTC building, I was greeted by an empty reception desk. I glanced around, started down the hall on the right hoping to find somebody in one of the offices.

"Stop right there," a deep voice behind me ordered. "This is a restricted area."

I spun around to face a heavyset guy in crisp green army fatigues. Clean-shaven, severe crewcut, gray around the temples. Looked like he had a hard fifty years on him. Name tag said "Grimm." It wasn't clear whether it was his name or a personality trait. He stood directly in front of the door, legs apart, arms crossed, with a square-jawed scowl that announced it would be futile to try anything. Like escaping, for instance.

"What do you think you're doing here?" More of an accusation than a question.

"I … I was looking for the receptionist."

"Took a few days leave since we're between sessions." He looked like he was about to pull a gun on me. Likely something semi-automatic. "You have a question. Ask it."

Jesus, this is a public building on a college campus, not the fucking Pentagon. Why is this guy being such an asshole? I managed a weak half-smile. "I was hoping I might look up something in your historical records."

"Off-limits. Our records are official government property. Classified. Authorized personnel only." He stepped around behind me, which caused me to have to pivot around to face him. He was now drill-sergeant close; I half expected him to give me a dressing down for being out of uniform. "And something tells me *you* aren't authorized."

"What about the Freedom of Information Act? Why would the historical records of an ROTC facility on a college campus be classified?"

"The FOIA only applies if you've got the proper paperwork and official permission to access the information in question. Which, if you had it, you'd have already shown me."

I closed my eyes, blew out a sigh. "Listen, I'm not interested in government secrets." I managed a friendly smile. He didn't return it. Maybe didn't recognize it. "I'm only trying to find out if someone bombed the ROTC building here back in 1970."

He narrowed his eyes. "Why, exactly, are you so interested in that particular information?"

"Um … it's research. I'm writing a book based on an incident like that happened at Carlyle during the student protests back then."

"An incident?" His frown brought into play a whole squadron of creases in his face. "This is a federal facility. If an attack as destructive as you say happened here, it could be considered an act of terrorism. The case would still be open."

"Really? After more than forty years?"

"Time doesn't come into play. Since the PATRIOT Act, there's no longer a statute of limitations on terrorist acts."

I sucked in a breath. "Look, I'm not writing about terrorism, and it's not an exposé. It's a *novel*. A piece of fiction."

217

"Doesn't matter what you call it. It won't get you access to any military records. Gotta go through channels." He smirked, likely the closest he ever came to a smile.

I held up my hands in surrender. "Forget it. I was just curious." I pivoted away from him in my best imitation of a crisp military about-face and marched out the door.

He shouted after me, "Anything you write about this government facility will have to be cleared by us."

I marched on.

Chapter 30

I fed the meter again then headed over to the impressive new student union to see about getting some lunch and a beer. The way my luck was going, though, Carlyle would turn out to be an alcohol-free campus and the food court would be shut down for spring break.

The directory on the wall, just inside the main entrance, indicated that the Coyote Tap and Grill was one floor down. I ran my finger down the list and noticed The Cascadian. College yearbooks had gone the way of the dinosaur, but I figured this could be the student newspaper. A facepalm moment for sure. Should have thought about that already. The student paper just might be a place where I stood a chance of finding something about an ROTC bombing more than forty years ago. If they had accessible archives. Worth a try; I had nothing to lose but time.

Near the end of the corridor, I stopped at the office with *The Cascadian* boldly displayed above the door. Looked to be the campus newspaper all right, given the slogan just below the name: "Everything you want to know and then some."

The door was ajar. I nudged it open farther to reveal a thin guy with a scraggly beard and glasses lounging behind a cluttered desk. This would be Gabriel Hunter, Editor, if the nameplate on his desk were to be believed. Younger than me, a senior probably. Maybe a grad student.

I stepped into the room. "Got a minute?"

The guy grinned and stood up. "Sure as hell do. I hate doing spreadsheets." He gestured to the papers fanned out on his desk. "Anytime I can avoid crunching numbers, I'm a happy guy."

I extended my hand. "Nick Castle."

He shook it. "Gabe Hunter. Here, sit down." He lifted the pile of debris from a chair near his desk, set it on the floor.

As I eased into the chair, I noticed the stacks of back issues of *The Cascadian* against one wall.

Hunter followed my gaze. "Yeah, I know. It"s a fuckin' disaster area. I try to keep things neater during the school year. I'm in the process of weeding out anything worth keeping from all the crap that's been accumulated over the year. Some of it's interesting. Most isn't." He offered me a warm smile. "So, how can I help you?"

"I'm researching an event that happened on the Carlyle campus over forty years ago. I thought you might have saved issues from as far back as 1970."

Hunter winced. "Sorry, man, back issues that old are stored in the restricted archives at the library. You have to go there and use their in-house computers."

"Yeah. I was just there. They're in the middle of upgrading the computer system. No access 'til sometime next week." I stood.

Gabe nodded his sympathy. Then his eyes lit up. He held up his hand, index finger extended. "Wait a sec."

I plopped back down.

"We do have a shitload of old photos here in the office. One of the volunteers spent a month categorizing them all. They go *way* back." Hunter ambled over to one of the large filing cabinets, shoved aside a stack of papers with his foot, and pulled out the bottom drawer. "We're thinking of running a nostalgic pic and caption in each issue next year. You know, to try to reinforce the idea that Carlyle has a history beyond the football team's current won-lost record." He dropped down to a knee and shuffled through a bunch of files. "Ah, here it is." He stood and toted a folder bursting with photographs over to his desk. Written boldly on the folder with a thick black felt pen: "The '70s."

He laid the folder between us on the desk. "What are we looking for exactly?"

"There was supposed to be a bombing of the ROTC building during the campus unrest in 1970."

"Wow. Really?" Hunter handed me half the stack. "Let's go through these. You never know."

We shuffled through the images in silence. Apparently, most Carlyle students in the Seventies were either hippies or trying to look like them—lots of long hair, several huge afros, paisley, tie-dye shirts, miniskirts, bellbottoms, and granny glasses. I'd seen these styles in old movies. Maybe cool at the time, but borderline silly in retrospect. Well, maybe not the miniskirts or the no-bra look. The only buildings I saw served as backdrops for something else. This search was shaping up as another waste of time.

"Dude, we might be in luck. I found some ROTC stuff." Hunter slid a few of the photos over to me: Army ROTC students in formation, performing military drills, even a bunch

221

of them throwing their hats in the air—like at the Army-Navy football games Dad and I always watched on TV. No help though. I slumped back in the chair.

"Well now, what have we *here*?" Hunter grinned at me and handed over a couple of grainy black-and-white photos showing a building being consumed by a raging fire.

"I gotta admit it's a building on fire, but it could be any building on the campus." I checked the backs of the photos. Same generic scrawl on both: "Campus Fire." I handed them back to Hunter.

"No, no. Look closer." Hunter slid one back toward me, pointing to the edge of a wooden sign just visible in the right foreground of one of the photos. I could just make out "ROT" still in the frame.

"Fire like that sure could have been the result of an explosion," Hunter said.

Christ. The ROTC building did burn down here back in the Seventies. I stared at the image, stuck in purgatory between excitement and disappointment. All I could manage was a soft, "Yeah."

Hunter slid the photo from my grasp. "Here, I'll make a copy of these two for you." He trudged through the mess to a copier in the corner of the room. "It won't be very good quality. They're bad prints in the first place." He placed a photo on the copier window and closed the top.

"No, it's fine for my purposes."

Hunter pulled the second mage from the photocopier, strode back, and handed me the copies.

I folded them in half and slid them into my messenger bag. "Thanks, Gabe, I owe you." I started for the door, then turned back. "How about I buy you a beer? I'm thinking of heading down to the Coyote Tap."

"Sounds great, man. Might help clear the dust from my throat after going through this chaos." He gestured to the piles of paper all over the floor.

◆ ◆ ◆

The Tap offered a curious selection of craft beers. Gabe suggested I try one called, "Vlad the Imp Aler." I rolled my eyes.

He grinned. "I know, the name is a bit too cute. But, trust me, it's tasty … if you like ale. It actually won a medal at the Great American Beer Festival."

I chuckled. "In spite of the name."

"Probably. Maybe because of it. Who knows? Anyhow, it's good."

"Why not?" I shrugged. "A chance to live dangerously."

Gabe ordered.

I paid.

We settled into a booth along the wall. Where we both took long pulls of Vlad as if we'd just crawled in from a week-long desert trek. It wasn't bad.

Hunter put down his bottle, looked over at me, and slapped his forehead. "Jesus, what's the matter with me. Listen, man, if you really want to know what happened around here back in the Seventies, you need to talk to Groovy Greg."

"Groovy Greg?" I couldn't stifle a snicker. First Vlad the Imp Aler and now Groovy Greg? What was next, a barmaid named Carrie Okie?

Hunter chuckled. "Yeah, I know. His real name is Martin Greggerson. But he goes by Groovy Greg or some variation of it. The Groovester and Groovy are also favorites."

"You're kidding, right?"

He raised an eyebrow, shook his head. "Nope, it's all part of his eternal hippie image. Apparently, he showed up in Sinclair sometime in the Sixties, and he's been a fixture around the Carlyle campus ever since. If anyone knows what was *happenin'* here on campus in the Seventies, Groovy does. No one believes all the shit he claims to have done, but the truth is, he's probably hiding a hell of a lot more than he lets on."

"I suppose it can't hurt to talk to him. Where can I find this guy?"

"He owns a little bar a few blocks off campus called Rocky Raccoon's."

"That sounds familiar." I tilted my head to the side, searching through Dad's Beatles archive in my head. He was a big fan. I became one.

"An old Beatles tune," Hunter said. "From their *White Album*, I think. A bit before our time." He sketched out the directions to the bar on a napkin and handed it to me.

When we finished our ales, we both rose and shook hands.

"Thanks for the Vlad, Nick."

"No, thank *you*." I patted my messenger bag. "And for turning me on to Groovy Greg. He sounds like someone I want to talk to for sure."

"No problem, man. But I should warn you. Word around campus is that all the drugs have taken their toll. You can draw your own conclusions when you see him." He rolled his eyes.

224

"But he's harmless, and he's been part of the local scene since before my *parents* went to Carlyle. At least he should be entertaining."

Chapter 31

Rocky Raccoon's turned out to be a hole-in-the-wall three and a half blocks from the campus. One step through the door and I was engulfed by the familiar smell of greasy bar food and stale beer. Reminded me I still hadn't eaten lunch, and I was starving. The sparse display of hard liquor bottles behind the bar told me the tavern served mostly beer. Not surprising. A college bar, after all.

The walls were blanketed with framed concert posters and album covers from an era long past. Jimi Hendrix, the Beatles, Bob Dylan, and the Doors I knew pretty well. Dad's taste in music had become mine. A huge Grateful Dead poster took me back to the time—I was probably fifteen or sixteen—when Dad and I hiked the foothills of Shoat Valley, and he beguiled me with tales of the long, strange Dead Head phenomenon.

Dad. My heart plummeted into my gut, a duck shot in mid-flight. Was this going to be my life going forward? Was I ever going to get past debilitating grief and sadness whenever I thought of him? Maybe. Probably. I focused on the smiling image of Sophie in my head. Better.

The barstools were empty and only two of the six small tables were occupied. I coasted by two coeds drinking coffee at a table near the door. The collected works of Walt Whitman and T. S. Eliot lay open on the table in front of them. Since Carlyle's spring term had just ended, I guessed they were probably working on a paper to make up an Incomplete. Been there.

A couple of older guys played gin rummy at a table against the back wall. Barflies direct from central casting

"What can I get you?" a smoky female voice behind me asked.

Startled, I spun around to the welcoming smile of the forty-something, blonde bartender. "Well, I suddenly feel like a cheeseburger and a beer, ma'am."

"Comin' right up. But that 'ma'am' stuff won't fly here. Call me Annie, *not* Ann."

"Pleased to meet you, *Annie*. I'm Nick."

"I was named after 'Dreamboat Annie.' The Heart song?" She gestured to a poster near the door, looked at me, shook her head. "Bet you don't have any idea who Heart is."

"You'd lose that bet." I gestured to the poster. "Love that album, especially 'Crazy on You.'"

She grinned. "I'm impressed. Not many people your age know much about classic rock."

"My dad was a big fan of classic rock and blues. It kinda rubbed off on me."

"Well, Nick, got Bud and Bud Lite on tap and more choices along the back there." Annie gestured to the row of beer bottles in front of the large bar mirror. "Personally, I prefer Manny's Pale Ale. It's local, and if you haven't tried it, you should."

"Sold." If nothing else I was getting a handle on the local craft beer scene.

Annie pulled a bottle out of the refrigerator under the bar, popped the top, and set it and a glass in front of me.

I waved away the glass. "Bottle's fine." I studied it, then offered something between a laugh and a chuckle. "Can't go wrong with something that claims it's a 'darn tasty beer' right on the label."

She glanced over and winked. "Have your cheeseburger up in a sec. Comes with fries, unless you got somethin' against 'em."

"Fries'd be great." I watched Annie slap a patty on the grill, dump fries into the wire basket, and ease it into the hot oil. "I was hoping to be able to talk with Groovy Greg. Is he around?"

She broke into a crooked smile. "My dad should be back in a few minutes. Went out to run an errand and grab a smoke. Illegal to smoke inside a bar anymore. Even when you own it."

She flipped the burger, laid a slice of cheese on it, and placed both halves of a bun face down on the grill. "So, what do you want to talk to him about?"

"Well, I hear he's something of an expert on what happened around here in the Seventies." I took another pull on the bottle.

Annie laughed. "Hell, in his mind, he's the world's greatest expert on everything from politics to rock and roll back in the day. Why are you so interested in somethin' that took place here over forty years ago? You a reporter?" She pulled the sizzling basket of fries out of the oil, shook it, and dumped the fries into a red plastic basket.

"Nope, nothing like that. I'm working on a novel that's loosely based on something that might have happened on the Carlyle campus back then."

She nestled the cheeseburger next to the fries, picked up the basket with one hand, deftly snatched squeeze bottles of ketchup and mustard with the other, and laid it all out in front of me.

I squirted ketchup on the burger and dug in.

"Well, speak of the devil." Annie nodded toward an old man shuffling through the door.

My mouth full of burger, I twisted around on the barstool for a better look.

"My ears are burnin'." The old guy chuckled. No more than five-six, he had to weigh at least two hundred pounds. Unruly white hair was trying to escape from under a worn red-and-black tam-o'-shanter, and his equally unkempt beard was just as snowy white. In the middle of all that hair, I could just make out a pair of red-rimmed, washed-out blue eyes—the look of someone who had taken a lot of drugs in his time, likely some quite recently. Underneath the beard, a mostly red Grateful Dead tie-dyed T-shirt that didn't quite manage to cover his potbelly, baggy rust-colored cargo shorts, and red, high-top tennis shoes completed the ensemble. Santa Claus on acid.

Annie spoke first. "Dad, this is Nick ..." She turned to me.

"Castle."

She shifted back to Groovy. "Nick Castle, and he'd like to talk to you."

I grabbed a napkin and wiped my hands.

"*Would* he?" He shuffled over to me and shook my hand.

"I'm honored to meet you, sir," I said.

"First of all, everyone calls me *Groovy*. Got that?"

I nodded.

He eyed me up and down. "And second, I charge a hundred bucks an interview."

I didn't have a response to that one.

Annie laughed. "First of all, Dad, Nick isn't a reporter. And second, nobody's wanted to interview you in twenty years."

He broke into a huge grin. "Just fuckin' with ya, umm …" He furrowed his brow.

"Nick," I reminded him.

"Right … *Nick*." Groovy stepped behind the bar and pulled out a bottle of Manny's Pale Ale, popped the top, and took a long pull. He gestured with his bottle toward mine. "I see me and you got similar tastes, son. So, what would a young fella like you want to talk to this particular old fart about?" He shuffled out from behind the bar and motioned me over to a table off to the side.

I collected my beer and basket and followed. "I'm trying to gather some information about an event that may have happened here back in 1970."

Groovy tilted his head back, closed his eyes. "By then, the rebel spirit of the Sixties was startin' to wind down. Wasn't a good time, you know? Lotta sad memories. In the late Sixties, we was as close to a full-on revolution as I ever saw. Not only that, the early Seventies was when the Beatles finally broke up for real." He sighed as he stared at a *Sgt. Pepper's Lonely Hearts Club Band* poster.

230

Groovy returned his gaze to me, "Okay, 1970." He shook his head slowly. "That's the year Janis and Jimi both died." He gestured to the huge poster of Hendrix performing at Woodstock and fell silent.

I dipped a fry in ketchup, letting Groovy proceed at his own pace.

The old man stared into space. "I traveled with Jimi in the early years. Was there with him at Woodstock." He let out a long deep sigh. "Man, that was some awesome trippin'. I 'member one time … in Chicago, I think. Jimi was doin' a gig with Zeppelin and Santana. No wait, not Santana. Maybe Jefferson Airplane. Anyway, lots of big names were there. Point is, backstage after every show, there musta been twenty or thirty chicks wanting to get their hands on anybody associated with one o' the bands." He gave me a sly grin. "All I had to do was to tell 'em I was a personal friend of Jimmy Page and Robert Plant, and I had all the pussy I could handle. Wasn't no lie, neither. I was tight with both of 'em."

"Impressive."

Groovy blew out a breath, shut his eyes. "Son, you can't begin t' imagine what it was like back then."

Annie arrived to clear my food basket and replace the two empty Manny's bottles with fresh ones. She shook her head in mock disgust. "*Imagine* is the right word for sure. Your imagination is where most of your memories come from, you old reprobate." She lifted Groovy's tam, kissed the top of his bald head, plopped his hat back in place, and sauntered back to the bar.

He winked at me. "She don't know the half of it, son. Some things you just don't wanna be relatin' in front of a

231

woman … 'specially your daughter. Trust me, the things I haven't told Annie would fill one a them fuckin' coffee-table books. Lots of great memories. Lots." He stared off into space for several seconds then came back to earth. "But you were inquirin' about somethin' that happened *here* … on the Carlyle campus, right?"

Great. I wouldn't have to steer him back from his rock-and-roll memories. "Yeah, I'm trying to find out if something I read about actually happened here … in the spring of 1970."

"Spit it out, boy. What's this *somethin'* you're talkin' 'bout?"

"Well I heard that during the campus unrest in May of that year"—I took a deep breath—"a student named Braden Delaney allegedly bombed the ROTC building at Carlyle … to protest the Vietnam War."

"Man, I'm here to tell ya, those were scary times for sure. It wasn't just the war we were protestin'. Still fightin' for civil rights back then, even though all kinds of discrimination were officially against the law." Air quotes around officially. "And the government was total bullshit then. Even though he denied it in his famous speech, Tricky Dick Nixon turned out to be exactly the damn crook we always knew he was."

"So, there *was* a protest movement at Carlyle."

"Oh yeah. Nothin' that hogged all the headlines like at Kent State or Berkeley, but there was lots of folks caught up in the whole "No-More-War" thing. Bad times for sure. Really bad."

"But what about the Carlyle ROTC building? Did someone blow it up in the spring of that year?"

"Could have. Can't really say for sure what was specifically goin' on here at Carlyle in the *spring* of 1970, though."

"You mean you don't remember?"

"Nah, it's not that. I mean, I think I heard somethin' about what happened to the ROTC building, but I didn't learn about it until after I got back to town. See, that particular spring I wasn't in Sinclair much. In those days I was following the Grateful Dead on tour back east. Hundreds of us showed up at every damn venue." He leaned in closer. "We were high the whole time. The *whole* time." A smile crept over his face; Groovy was lost in his memories again. "Good times." He closed his eyes and bobbed his head as if to the rhythm of some long-ago rock ballad.

"So, you weren't actually *here* around the middle of May then?"

"Sorry, son, the only way I'd a been here is if the Dead were givin' a concert on the Carlyle campus. And as I kinda recall, we were all back east around then … or the Midwest. Hell, coulda been anywhere … 'cept Sinclair."

I wasn't sure if I felt frustrated that Groovy couldn't confirm the bombing, or if I was relieved he couldn't verify that it never happened. Maybe I was just worn out trying to keep up with the old man's meandering narrative.

"Wish I could be more help, umm …" He squinted at me.

"Nick."

"Right, Nick. I'm not so good with names. What were we talkin' about again?"

"The bombing of the ROTC building at Carlyle."

"Right. Well, I *do* know that they put up a new ROTC buildin' on campus. So somethin' musta happened to the old one. The new building went up … around the time of the big Bicentennial celebration, I think. Lotta patriotic hoopla about it as I recall."

I nodded. Six or so years after it was blown up seemed about the right amount of time to wade through all the bureaucratic red tape and get the thing rebuilt.

Groovy slapped his hand on the table. "Damn, I know exactly who you ought to talk to, son. She'd know all about that protestin' for sure. She and her boyfriend were right smack in the middle of it."

"She?"

"Yeah, Channing … Chavon—"

I forced down the lump in my throat. "Cheryl?"

"Yeah, that sounds 'bout right. Cheryl. I'm pretty sure Chavon was one of us Dead Heads." He glanced over at Annie, then back at me. "Damn that Chavon chick could suck the chrome off a trailer hitch." Groovy shook his head slowly, let out a sigh.

I wasn't about to tell him I'd heard Willie Nelson deliver almost the same line in an old movie. Not now. "This Cheryl you mentioned … could she have been Cheryl *Stevens*?" My heart impersonated a frenzied bongo player.

He stared out into space. "Yeah, could be 'Stevens,' I guess."

"Are you saying she still lives around here after all these years?"

"Not here in Sinclair. She got herself a place a ways outta town. Might still be there, I guess. Lives out there with her son

… at least she used to." He took a healthy swallow from his bottle.

I followed suit. My throat seemed to be full of dust. I could be dangerously close to finding out the truth about Dad once and for all. "Way I heard it, Cheryl was Braden Delaney's girlfriend. Do you know if they're still together?"

"Dunno. But it's been my experience that most couples didn't last long back then." He picked up his beer and set it back down without taking a drink. "I figured me and my Janie would be paired up our whole life. But it didn't work out." He shrugged. "Love the one you're with, I guess. But it was my fault. Too many drugs. Too many other …." Groovy's eyes clouded over.

This time I had to bring him back. I needed an answer. "Groovy? Sir? Excuse me!"

Groovy blinked back to reality. "Oh. Umm, what were you sayin'?"

"Do you think Braden Delaney still lives here … with Cheryl Stevens?"

Groovy sighed. "You gotta pay attention, ah …"

"Nick."

"Right … *Nick.* I just got finished tellin' you he was livin' out there with her last I heard. Can't say if he still is though."

An icy wave flowed through me, and I grabbed the edge of the table to steady myself. This changed *everything*.

If Groovy was to be believed, both Cheryl and Braden were real people. Even if Delaney wasn't still in the area, there was a damn good chance he'd lived here with Cheryl long after Dad had arrived in Shoat Valley. If Braden had been living with

Cheryl in Washington all these years, he sure as hell didn't go to Honduras. But wherever he'd been living, he wasn't Jim Castle. I did my best to work past the gleeful puppy jumping up and down inside me.

"Do you have an address for Cheryl? I'd really like to talk to her. To both of them."

"Son, if I ever knew it, I sure as hell don't remember it now. I ain't much better with numbers than I am with names. Never was." His eyes fogged over once again.

I'd try the Internet, or a local phone book, something … anything, but damn it, I was going to connect with Cheryl Stevens. I threw down the last of my beer. "Thank you so much for taking the time to talk with me, Groovy. You've been a big help."

I stood up, offered my hand.

Groovy didn't seem to notice. He nodded in my direction, but his eyes focused elsewhere. I didn't know where the old man thought he was at the moment, but it wasn't sitting alone at a table in Rocky Raccoon's.

I stopped at the counter and took out my wallet.

Instead of a bill, Annie handed me a slip of paper with directions to Cheryl Stevens' place. "Used to see her around town every once in a while. Played the clubs around here for years. Great piano player; girl could sing, too. Haven't heard anything about Cheryl in a few years, but this is where she used to live. Twenty miles or so from here. Best I can do."

My luck was definitely changing. "Thanks, Annie, you just saved me a lot of research. So how much do I owe you for lunch?"

"On the house, Nick." She nodded toward Groovy; I followed her gaze. "You've made my dad's day. He's a whole lot happier lost in the past than he is with what's going on right in front of him."

The old man seemed to be silently reliving memories of lost friends and fantasies.

Annie sighed. "It's what he gets for doing all those drugs for god-knows-how-many years straight. At this point, I don't think it matters if what he's remembering really happened or not."

"Maybe you're right. But he sure looks the part."

She laughed. "He figures his crazy hippie persona sucks in the customers. It did for a lot of years, and he was in heaven. A bona fide local celebrity. But you can see how effective that image is these days." She gestured to the nearly empty bar. "I don't mind, though. I suppose it helps him believe he's still the same wild counterculture icon he was back in the day."

I smiled. "He's interesting, ya gotta give him that."

Annie smiled over at her father. "He is what he is." Her voice cracked a little. "I'm just thankful my dad's still around."

I felt a catch in my throat. My dad wasn't.

When I stepped out of the dimness of Rocky Raccoon's, the bright sun exploded in front of me. I whipped out my sunglasses, headed to the car, and took a quick inventory of what I'd learned so far. One, there may or may not have ever been a hippie commune called "Sadie's Farm" near Medford. Two, a smuggler who sometimes went by the alias "Lobo" had spent some time in Port Orford. Three, an ROTC building on

237

the Carlyle campus was replaced after burning down around the time Dad's story indicated. And four, a real person named Braden Delaney and his real girlfriend, Cheryl Stevens, might still live near Sinclair.

If Cheryl and Braden were still together, I'd be able to throw all the other "evidence" out. If Braden Delaney was *still alive,* he sure as hell wasn't Jim Castle. Good thing I was too grown-up, or I might have broken into a Snoopy dance right there on the sidewalk.

I settled into the front seat, squeezed my eyes shut, and eased out a sigh. My anxiety about Dad slowly flowed from my body, a disappointed apparition moving on to haunt someone else. I deserved to savor the moment. There could be several explanations of how Dad knew so much about Braden Delaney. Could be I was about to find out. But I really didn't care at the moment. Right now, I was dead tired. But it was a good tired.

I'd find a nice, safe motel here in Sinclair, and drive out to Cheryl Stevens' place in the morning. Cheryl—and hopefully Braden himself—would be able to provide crucial details about Delaney's story that I might be able to use. My researching-a-novel cover story didn't sound so bogus anymore.

Chapter 32

I found a Best Western motel just off the highway, a few miles north of Sinclair. You know what you're getting with Best Western. Nice enough place, nice enough room. No surprises.

Once I was settled in, I charged my cell phone. Wanted it at a hundred percent when I called Sophie later. When it reached capacity, I checked the clock radio on the nightstand: 5:07. Too early to call her, but not too early to grab something to eat.

Turns out, meals become a major focus when you're traveling by yourself and living out of motel rooms. Probably shouldn't have come as a surprise. After all, when we were kids, on family vacations, eating at restaurants was a highlight for Shelby and me. But things were different now. I wasn't a kid. And I was eating alone.

I'd noticed a Red Lobster on the way in. The best thing about chain restaurants is the menu is the same, and you can usually find one within walking distance of a motel. At Red Lobster it's possible to get a combo plate of seafood where everything on it is deep-fried but the sauces. Tempting, but no. I went with the lobster alfredo. Tasty, if a little rich, and there was a lot of it. I ate as much as I could and had the rest boxed up so I could accidentally leave it behind in the motel room refrigerator when I checked out tomorrow.

Back in the room, overfull and tired, I knew there was a chance I might fall asleep. So, I set the alarm on my cell phone for 7:30 p.m. That's when I'd call Sophie. I lay back on the bed with the TV remote, flipped through every single channel available, twice. Found nothing more interesting than a *Gunsmoke* rerun. Twenty minutes into the episode, I dozed off.

When the alarm woke me, I stood, stretched, and splashed cold water on my face. Then I climbed onto the bed, my back against the fake headboard, and dialed Sophie's cell. She picked up on the second ring, and her "hello" was enough to send a warm rush through my body. Before we knew it, we'd talked for nearly three hours. Like teenagers. How had that happened? By the time we hung up, I didn't remember all we talked about. What I did remember was that I was happier than I'd ever been in my life. I could almost see Dad sitting right there on the only chair in the dark motel room, smiling, approving. Thinking of him caused a chill to ooze slowly down my spine, but in the end, I drifted off to sleep with a smile on my face. Sophie.

◆　◆　◆

In the morning, I resisted the urge to call her, just to tell her good morning. I took a quick shower, shaved. I rummaged through my bag until I found a clean shirt. I wanted to look my best for the meeting with Cheryl Stevens.

I didn't know what to expect from her, but I was excited to meet her—not to mention Braden Delaney—to get a handle on what really happened all those years ago at Carlyle. But what mattered most was that a living Braden Delaney meant he couldn't be Jim Castle. Simple as that.

Then, why was I still feeling anxious about what I might discover? I tried to bury any remaining doubts, but they still crouched in the back of my mind, ready to pounce. The tightness in my chest caught me by surprise. I switched to thoughts of Sophie and immediately broke into a whole-face grin.

By midmorning, I was back on the road. The GPS talked me through the twenty-seven miles from the Best Western to 2 Arcadian Lane, the address Annie had given me for Cheryl Stevens. Fifteen minutes after I left the highway and turned onto a two-lane rural road, I passed through the center of the happy little village of Graybow—a gas station/market, a bar, and a church clustered together on the side of the road like a welcoming committee. After that, except for the unending lush green forest on both sides of the road, I didn't see much of interest.

Then I did.

At the turn onto Arcadian Lane, I spied a single mailbox in the distance. One mailbox most likely meant only one residence on the lane. As I drew nearer, I could make out "B. Delaney" in bold red letters. My pulse sped up. So, Cheryl *was* still living with Braden. I pulled over to the side of the road, took in a slow, deep breath, and eased it back out.

I punched off the radio and listened to the purr of the Prius's idling engine while I stared at the mailbox. Written right in front of me in red was proof that Dad's manuscript wasn't an autobiography. No more unwarranted suspicion. I felt the anxiety drifting from my body like a lonely dark cloud. I was free. I'd stay with my cover of researching a novel. No way to tell how much Dad's manuscript was based on fact, if that even mattered anymore.

I eased through the strobing sunlight and shadow and focused on finding Delaney's house, which had to be somewhere in this abundant evergreen landscape. I'd gone nearly a mile before I spotted a two-story, white clapboard house well back from the road, nestled among the fir, hemlock, and cedar. I didn't want to startle Braden and Cheryl—they probably chose this remote spot for its privacy. Made sense, since Braden would have to keep a low profile once he snuck back into the area after his years in exile. If he even spent any years in exile. The crunch of the tires on the gravel driveway guaranteed that no one could sneak up unnoticed.

I didn't know what to expect. Was the tightness in my stomach because I was excited, or was I a little frightened? Of what? That Delaney would chase me off with a shotgun? Course not. Delaney wouldn't be a crusty old codger in his dotage quite yet. According to Dad's manuscript, Braden was twenty in 1970. He and Cheryl would be in their early sixties.

I pulled up next to a charcoal gray Accord in front of a house that was in excellent shape. A lot of work had been done to maintain and update it. I noticed the lawn was freshly cut and trimmed, and someone with a green thumb had created a multicolored hedgerow of rose bushes and flowering shrubs all along its perimeter.

Just before I killed the engine, I caught a glimpse of someone pulling aside a curtain in one of the upstairs rooms.

I was two steps up the front stairs when an attractive blonde padded onto the porch in a flowered smock, black leggings, and white crew socks. I guessed she was in her thirties and at least six months pregnant. She brushed a strand of blonde hair from her cheek.

I offered a warm smile. "Hi, my name is Nick Castle. Is your father home?"

"My *father*?" Hearty laugh.

Her reaction caused me to recoil enough that I dropped down a step. "I'm sorry. I didn't mean to assume, I just … I … so, Braden Delaney isn't your father?"

"Nope." She chuckled. "He's my *husband*. I'm *Mrs.* Delaney, but everyone calls me 'Lizzie.'"

"Okay, Lizzie, now that I'm feeling like a complete idiot, do you think it would be possible for me to talk with your *husband* … before I dig myself in any deeper?"

She winked. "No problem. You'll find him around back. He's converted the garage into his workshop." She tilted her head toward the right side of the house. Her eyes widened, as did her smile. "He'll be glad to see you. We can always use the money, especially now." She patted her bulging tummy. "Whoops, the little fella is getting restless." She glanced back at me. "It's gonna be a boy."

"Congratulations."

She beamed.

"Thank you, Lizzie." I nodded, just short of a bow, and descended the steps backward, a court jester backing away from a queen.

I made my way around the house and headed for an open door on the side of the garage. I had no idea what money Lizzie

243

was talking about, but I wasn't about to let that distract me. Not this close to meeting the real Braden Delaney. There had to be a thirty-year difference between him and Lizzie, not that that mattered—although I was impressed that Delaney was up to fathering a child at his age. More important, though, if Delaney was married to Lizzie, where did that leave his longtime love, Cheryl Stevens?

As I approached the open side door of the garage/studio, I noticed several cabinetry projects in various stages of completion, every one of them impressive. Something classical played in the background. Maybe Mozart. Sophie would know. She was a fan of classical music.

I stepped onto the concrete block that served as a doorstep into the studio, then backed right down again, where I stood frozen, slack-jawed. *This* was Braden Delaney? No. Not possible.

The Braden Delaney who glanced up at me was twenty years younger than he should have been. What the hell? Not only that, he was Black. Delaney had a dark mocha complexion, a neatly trimmed coal-black beard. He was good-looking, a couple of inches taller than me, and a hell of a lot more muscular. His salt-and-pepper dreadlocks were pulled back into a ponytail that exploded like fireworks from the back of his head.

My brain was revving full bore. Okay, the Braden Delaney of the manuscript must be *this* one's father. That meant the elder Delaney was probably Black, too. A fact Dad hadn't mentioned in the manuscript. But then, Jim Castle was colorblind when it came to people.

Delaney stepped out to where I was still held fast by some invisible magnet. "You okay, man? Can I get you a glass of water? You look like you're about to pass out."

Despite the brain buzzes and adrenalin rushes, I managed to force a smile. "Oh, sorry … no, I'm fine."

"Well, then come on in to the shop." He gestured for me to follow, and I shuffled inside behind him. "Hope you don't mind me workin' while we talk. I have to get a last coat of varnish on this job, so it'll be good and dry by tomorrow. Tight deadline."

He sat back down on a stool and dipped his brush into a gallon can. The air was permeated with the smell of varnish and some kind of cleaning solvent. Turpentine?

I was impressed by his precise brushstrokes along the top of the cabinet. "It's beautiful. What kind of wood is that?"

"Glad you like it. I'm using cherry on this one. Not as heavy as oak." He reached over to the disc player next to his workbench and turned down the volume. "It's a custom cabinet for a TV and sound system. Used to be somethin' like this would have to be oak or maple to support the heavy load. Back when a television weighed about the same as a Buick." He grinned, gestured to the cabinet. "The specs on this one had to be very precise, so it'll fit in a limited space. You lookin' for something like this? I can turn it around in a few days if you're in a hurry."

"Well, actually I—"

He glanced over at me. "Damn, I'm forgetting my manners. You gotta forgive me, man. I'm goin' way too fast here. We haven't even met." He grabbed a rag, wiped his hands, and held his right one out to me. "I'm Brady Delaney."

I shook it. "Nick Castle." Time for subtlety. "So … 'Delaney' is kind of an unusual name. Irish?"

He narrowed his eyes at me. "Do I *look* Irish?"

I tried to respond, but nothing came out except random vowels.

He held up his hand. "Chill, man. Just a messin' with ya. My full name is Braden Charles Delaney, Junior. A bit too snooty for my taste. I'm more of a 'Brady,' don't you think?

I nodded, smiled. "Still, it's certainly not a name you see often."

Delaney shrugged. "Mama named me after my ol' man." He rolled his eyes. "But enough about me. You don't need my whole damn biography."

I winced at his dismissal of the subject. He had no idea how important that information was to me.

"So, I understand you're interested in a project. Matching end tables, wasn't it? No problem, I can custom make you just about any piece of furniture you can name. I guarantee all my work."

I saw the hopefulness in his eyes.

He widened his smile. "Plus, since we're pretty far from civilization way out here, I offer free delivery."

"Sounds like a good deal." I waved my arm to encompass all the pieces in view. "And I'm really impressed with the quality of your work. But I'm afraid that's not why I'm here."

"Wait. You're *not* the guy who called about the end tables?"

"Afraid not." I cringed. "Sorry."

Delaney sucked in a breath through clenched teeth. "Then why are you *here*, man?"

"Um … actually, I'm researching a book based loosely on Braden Delaney and Cheryl Stevens. Including their role in the student protests at Carlyle back in 1970."

Delaney sat down, huffed out a sigh. He grabbed the brush balanced on the top of the varnish can and resumed coating the cabinet. All without looking at me. "So, you writin' some kind of history of the college?" He maintained perfectly even brushstrokes.

"Not a history, more of a *novel*. I was hoping to be able to talk to your dad and mom. Is your father around?"

He blew air through his nostrils like a bull about to charge. Then he looked away. "Nope."

So, the older Delaney must have passed away. I wasn't about to ask. We both faced a future without our fathers. Not an area either one of us would want to pursue. I tilted my head toward the house. "Um, do you think I might talk with your mother? Is she home?"

Delaney paused, studied me. He wasn't smiling. "Tell me again why're you so anxious to talk to her." He dipped his brush in the can, bent down, refocused on the work at hand.

"She might be the only person who knows what really happened at Carlyle back in the spring of 1970."

Delaney flipped the cabinet around in a half-circle as if it weighed nothing and began to varnish the back. "Up 'til about a month ago she lived in that house right behind you with me and Lizzie. Hell, it's *her* house. She lived here for almost thirty years. So did I, except for college and a stint in the Army to try

247

to get my head …" He glanced up at me, squeezed his eyes shut. "Damn. Sorry, man. I'm goin' off like any of this shit matters."

I waved away his concern. "No need to apologize. So, your mother has moved?"

"Yeah, she says relationships are hard enough without an old woman hangin' around to make things even more complicated. Lizzie and I tried to talk her out of it, but once my mama's made up her mind, ain't nothin' gonna change it."

I chuckled. "I'd really love to meet her, though. Do you have a current address for her?"

Delaney finished a stroke with a flourish, turned, and studied me. "Maybe. But no guarantee she'll talk to you. I'm not even sure I want her to." He balanced the brush back on the edge of the varnish can, narrowed his eyes at me. "She doesn't need some *stranger* diggin' up a bunch of sad memories."

I held both hands up, palms out. "No, no. I certainly don't want to do anything to upset her. I'm just hoping to have a friendly chat to find out if what I've read about her and your father is true or not. No one else has to know the details."

Delaney gave me a long, hard look. "Don't know why I should trust you, man. But you seem like a stand-up dude. I really doubt she's gonna be willing to talk to you about this shit. But I'll give her a call, see if she's up to it."

He wiped his hands, punched a couple of keys on his cell phone, and strode around the side of the shop out of earshot.

I stepped outside and took in a lungful of air that had no trace of varnish or turpentine.

When Brady reappeared, he was shaking his head in disbelief. "You're one lucky dude. She says for you to come by tomorrow around one-thirty. That work for you?"

248

"Really? One thirty'll be perfect."

"I'll let her know." Delaney picked up a notepad from his worktable and wrote down the address. "Mama bought a condo on Mercer Island, nice place overlooking Lake Washington." He tore off the sheet and handed it to me.

"Thanks, Brady. I really appreciate you helping me out." I stuck out my hand.

He shook it but held on. "It's all good, man. But if you upset her, things could get *bad* real fast. You feel me?" He stared me down.

I opened my mouth to respond, but before I could get the words out, he dropped my hand, spun around, and strode back into his workshop.

I'd been dismissed.

Chapter 33

All in all, a productive day, and it was only noon. Now I had a better handle on Braden Delaney, Sr.--one that made sense. After he returned to the states, he must somehow have managed to return to Sinclair and rejoin Cheryl Stevens. But I'd missed the window to meet him. So, the elder Delaney must have died here after he made his way back. He would have had to be looking over his shoulder the whole time, but Braden and Cheryl managed to make some kind of life together, raise a family.

Now that I was able to toss aside my embarrassing suspicion that *Dad* was Braden Delaney, I could focus on finding out more about the real Delaney's story from the person who knew him best.

Since Cheryl Stevens's condo on Mercer Island overlooked Lake Washington, that put it within Seattle proper. So, I decided to give the city another try. I took the on-ramp to I-90 that would take me west to Seattle and popped in Stevie Ray Vaughn's *Texas Flood* CD. As Stevie Ray belted out the first track, "Love Struck Baby," I felt a rush, as if the song were about *me*. And Sophie. Might as well admit it. I was lovestruck, and in such great spirits, I sang along. Badly off-key, but it didn't slow Stevie Ray down any.

By the time the last extended guitar chord faded out, I knew what to do. More than anything right now I wanted to be with Sophie again. I had something to celebrate, and I wanted to share it with her.

My appointment with Cheryl Stevens tomorrow wasn't until 1:30. I had nearly twenty-four hours to kill. God, how I wished Sophie were here with me. Why not give her a call? Short notice, but she *might* be able to get away. Assuming she wanted to.

I pulled into the gravel parking lot of a rundown restaurant-bar just off I-90. I was attracted less by the neon "Uncle Charley's" sign flickering randomly on the roof, than by the "Wi-Fi Hot Spot" notice in the front window. Good enough place to call Sophie and search the internet for a hotel.

I killed the engine and stared across the parking lot. Three cars in total. Mine made it a quartet. When the Uncle Charley's sign flashed from dark to bright, not all of the letters made the transition. The sides of the building were dotted with splotches of fire-engine red. Probably attempts to cover up graffiti. I figured that the whole place had probably once been a similar red, but now the peeling paint had faded to a washed-out Barbie pink.

I squeezed my eyes tight, took in a deep breath, let it out slowly. Dad's death, the worst thing that ever happened to me, was vying for space in my brain and my soul with Sophie, the best thing that ever happened to me. I was still a chip off the old block, always would be. I was still proud of that.

251

But meeting Sophie had caused my life to make a sharp turn in the right direction, away from my despair over Dad. Having her in my life softened the sense of abandonment and anger I'd been battling ever since Dad died. I found myself smiling for no reason. But it wasn't the same as laughing at a joke or giggling at the antics of a new puppy. The bliss came from somewhere deep inside me. My whole body smiled. This was brand-new to me. So, what did all this mean? Had the future become more important to me than the past? Was I moving on with my life? God, I hoped so.

I grabbed my messenger bag, crunched my way across the gravel to the front door of the bar, stepped inside. The place was awash in memorabilia, walls covered with tin beer signs mostly touting brands I'd never heard of. I recognized only one, the St. Pauli Girl's cleavage. In fact, a good portion of the wall posters seemed to have been chosen for their old-school pinup models. Easy-listening classic rock provided a low-volume background.

The only customers in the place were two old-timers at the bar playing liar's poker with the bartender. The bartender was dark-haired, bearded, portly, and jovial. One of the two old guys was short, bald, and wore a faded green Seahawks T-shirt. The other was white-bearded, a navy-and-teal Mariners cap pulled down almost to his bushy eyebrows. All three turned and stared at me as if I'd just landed my spaceship in the parking lot. I ordered a draft, paid, and took it to a table near the front window. I set the beer on the table, dropped my messenger bag next to it. I sat down and checked out the action at the bar.

Baldy groaned, drew a couple of dollar bills from his pocket, and slammed one on the bar. His companion chuckled and yanked his cap off, releasing a shock of snow-white hair. He removed a buck from inside his cap, tossed it on the bar, and slapped the cap back on his head. The bartender slid both dollars off the bar into the cash register.

I pulled out my cell and iPad, set them in front of me. Everything I needed, except for the Wi-Fi password. I looked over at the bartender, but before I said a thing, he waved a hand at the sign on the wall behind him. "Uncle Charley. One word, no caps," he said.

I nodded my thanks and signed in on the laptop. Then I called Sophie on my cell.

She answered on the second ring.

I got right to the point. "I'm thinking of staying over in Seattle for the weekend. But only if you can join me."

"Are you kidding? I'd love to. I've always wanted to spend some time in Seattle. But …"

My heart sank. "Uh-oh. But what?"

"I'm at work, Nick. I mean, I have the weekend off, and there shouldn't be any problem getting someone to cover for me tomorrow. But I can't just run off and leave Mom without arranging care. She's been doing much better lately, but I still need to check with her."

Forehead slap. "Christ, Sophie, I should have thought of that. I just got a little carried away. I miss you, and I have a reason to celebrate. I just wanted to raise a glass with *you*. That was just *selfish*. Sorry."

The line was silent.

Finally, she said, "You through apologizing?"

"Yeah." At least she couldn't see me blush.

"Okay, I'll talk to her about it. Call you right back."

I checked the availability of some of the nicer hotels in downtown Seattle for Friday and Saturday. Every one of them I tried was booked.

My cell rang. I grabbed it, anxious but hopeful.

"Mom said, and I quote, 'If you don't get your butt up to Seattle the fastest way possible, I'm cutting you out of the will.'"

We laughed in sync.

"She reminded me she has the number of a friend nearby if she needs anything."

My insides seem to vibrate. My heart was pounding faster than a heavy-metal drummer. It was all I could do to stop myself from shouting out loud. Instead, I said, "That's great. How soon can you get here?"

"Well, I can be out of here first thing in the morning, but I can't just hop a plane out of Port Orford International Airport, you know." She chuckled. "There's Southwest Oregon Regional in North Bend, but it looks like they route you through San Francisco to get to Seattle. That's just crazy. Looks like the best option is to drive a rental car to Portland, drop it off at the airport, and fly up from there. No point in having two cars in Seattle."

Oh my God, she'd already researched it. Felt like a hug. Still. "Damn, that's a hell of a drive. This is starting to feel like too much to ask."

"No, Nick, it's not. I miss you, too. I know you haven't even been gone two whole days, but I gotta tell you, hanging out with Leo at night just doesn't cut it anymore, now that I know what it can be like with … well, *you*."

"Trust me, I know what you mean."

"Let me see what I can book out of Portland, say midday tomorrow."

My heart still pumping like crazy. I sucked in a breath. "Wait. Better make it mid-afternoon. I have a 1:30 appointment with an old lady tomorrow. I'll try to get through it early, though."

"Another woman, huh? Should I be jealous?"

I laughed. "Seriously, her son is twice my age." I hesitated. "There is one other thing, though."

"Uh-oh."

"Not a huge deal. It's just that I'm getting nowhere finding a hotel in Seattle. Everything is booked for today and tomorrow."

"Of course they are. All the hotels are holding out for people who want to stay over the Memorial Day weekend, silly. They don't want to rent their rooms for only two nights on a three-day weekend. Tell them you want to book something for tonight through Monday. You'll be amazed at how fast they'll find something."

I shook my head. "I'm more amazed that a small-town girl like you even knows that stuff."

"Remember, Port Orford fancies itself a tourist destination. You live here, you learn that kinda stuff. Anyway, try it. If it doesn't work, we can stay somewhere else. I'd love to see Seattle. But you're the main attraction for me, writer-boy."

I savored the warmth rushing through me. It felt like love. Had to wait a beat before I could make words again. "I can't wait to see you, Sophie. I didn't know it was even possible to miss somebody this much."

"*Tell* me about it. But we better stop this kind of talk, mister. Sounds like you're in a public place, and I don't want you to embarrass yourself in front of strangers."

I glanced over at the two geezers at the bar. Baldy started making sloppy kiss sounds, while white beard clasped his hands to his heart mimicking a swoon. The bartender joined them in a robust group chortle.

"Good point," I whispered.

"Okay, you get us a room, and I'll book a flight."

"Deal. Let me know as soon as you book it. I'll do the same."

I punched off the call and waited for my heart to stop racing. Then I signaled the bartender for another draft. When he set the beer in front of me, he grinned down at me.

I pulled a five from my wallet.

He held up a palm. "On the house, son. Ain't been that much entertainment in this place for months." He winked, snatched up my empty bottle, and shuffled back to the bar.

Okay, I might have been a little … sappy on the phone. But I had more important things to do than care that my face was beet red. I went back to searching for a hotel. Finally, I found a room at the Mayflower Park, within walking distance of the famous Pike Place Market. The hotel wasn't one of those ultramodern all-glass-and-chrome edifices, but according to the pictures on the website, it had been completely refurbished, and it looked comfortable. It wasn't exactly cheap, but I didn't care what it cost. Tonight, I'd enjoy the hospitality of the Mayflower Park alone, but tomorrow I'd share my euphoria with Sophie in style.

By the time I finished my second beer, Sophie texted: *Booked on Alaska out of Portland. Arrive Sea-Tac tomorrow 3:14. Can't wait 2 see you.*

My response: *Perfect. Meeting with OL shd be over in plenty of time to pick u up at airport. Got us a hotel!* I added three grinning emojis.

I hit send. Then I sat back and savored the warmth that engulfed me.

Chapter 34

When Cheryl Stevens opened the door, she drew in a sharp breath and stared at me wide-eyed. Guess I wasn't what she expected. What the hell had Brady told her about me? Then again, she was hardly the frail, vulnerable old woman her son had implied.

After meeting Brady, I wasn't surprised Cheryl was Black, but I didn't expect her to be so striking. She looked much younger than her sixty-plus years. Svelte, maybe five-seven. Thick, ebony hair cut in a stylish bob settled just past her ears, and she wore a white silk blouse and a full-length black skirt with slashes of teal, red, and gold. And attached to the silver chain around her neck, a beautiful red-and-gold amulet that looked African. She must have been a real knockout in her younger days. Hell, she still *was*.

Her hand flew to her mouth, and she blinked. "Please forgive me, I didn't mean to leave you standing out in the hall." She stepped aside and motioned me past, her expression morphing into a warm smile. "I'm Cheryl Stevens. And I'm going to assume that you are the Nick Castle that Brady warned me about." She offered her hand, and I shook it. She had a surprisingly firm grip.

"Yes ma'am, I am. Thank you for taking the time to meet with me."

"I'm happy to. But since I'm planning to call you Nick, you can drop the 'ma'am. Please, call me Cheryl."

I nodded. "Deal."

She took my arm, and we entered a living room that was well lit by the sun streaming through a picture window that took up most of one wall. Two matching tan, leather couches, and an impressive green-and-gold upholstered armchair created a comfortable conversation area around a dark walnut coffee table. Looked like Brady's work.

She led me to one of the couches and motioned for me to sit. "I hope you haven't eaten. I've prepared a small lunch."

"Oh I … you didn't have to—"

"It shouldn't be a difficult decision, Nick." A wry look in her eye. "Either you've eaten, or you haven't."

The tingling at the back of my neck told me my cheeks were about to turn red. "Lunch would be great, thank you."

"You just relax here a minute, and I'll get us some freshly brewed herbal tea … unless you'd prefer coffee."

"Tea's fine." I sat back and surveyed my surroundings. Sunlight reflected off the polished surface of the baby grand piano next to the window, and a thriving split-leaf philodendron dominated the other side. A portrait of the Seattle skyline in bright sunlight took up a good portion of one wall, and another piece apparently by the same artist—the Seattle night sky as seen from the waterfront—complemented it from across the living room. Cheryl had passed through a small dining room into the kitchen, and I guessed the hallway beyond led to bedrooms and bathrooms. This place was a whole lot bigger than any condo I'd ever seen.

When she returned, bearing a tray with a ceramic teapot and two matching cups, I ran my hand across the surface of the coffee table. "This is beautiful."

"Yes, isn't it *nice*? Brady made it for me." She set the tray down on the table, eased down onto the couch across from me, then poured the tea. "Working with wood and building things is the way he's found his focus. It's a good choice. Even though he isn't using his engineering degree. Not directly anyway."

I huffed a laugh. "Yeah, I know what that's like. My degree's in English." I lifted my cup, sipped the tea.

She held hers in both hands, peering over the edge. "But I doubt you've come all the way to Seattle to hear me brag about my son."

"Well, no. Actually, I'm more interested in his father."

She studied me for several seconds, brow slightly furrowed. "Brady mentioned that. Something about an old manuscript?"

"Yeah, I think it's the first draft of a novel. My dad wrote it, but it's all about Braden Delaney."

She stared past me, as if at a ghost. When she refocused, she sucked in a breath. "Let's talk over lunch. I'm getting hungry. Hope you don't have any food allergies."

"Nope."

"Good." She rose and glided off to the kitchen again.

We hadn't even finished our tea. Did I say something to upset her? I felt a rumbling in my stomach. It wasn't hunger.

She returned, balancing two plates of food, and a small platter of cheeses and grapes.

I stood. "Let me help you with those."

She tilted her head to the side. "Does it look like I need help?" She set a plate in front of me and distributed the rest of the load onto the table as smoothly as if she were dealing cards.

I dropped back down. "I'm impressed."

"Don't be. You either learn how to carry several orders at once or your waitressing career is a short one."

I examined the plate in front of me—tuna salad on a crisp lettuce leaf, a warm dinner roll, and a ramekin of tomato soup. "This looks delicious."

"The proof is in the eating." She scooped up a forkful of tuna salad.

I tried the soup. It wasn't Campbell's. "So, you were a *waitress*?" I asked between bites. "I've heard you were a musician."

"I've been many things, Nick. Have to be when you're a single mother with a young son." She pulled apart a roll, buttered it. "I came out to Carlyle from Chicago on a music scholarship. My parents wanted me to become a concert pianist. That was my plan, too. But," she shrugged, "life."

"It can't have been easy," said Captain Obvious. I was never any good at small talk.

"No, it wasn't, Nick. But it all turned out fine in the end." She took a sip of tea. "After Brady went off to college, I tried my hand at playing the lounges and clubs around the state, but all the traveling wore me out. I still perform sometimes locally. And I give the occasional piano lesson. Helps keep me young."

"Well, I'd have to say it's working."

261

"That's sweet. Every woman enjoys a compliment, even one who's about to become a grandmother." She held up a hand to stop me before I could make another gratuitous comment. "How about you tell me why you're so interested in what happened at Carlyle over forty years ago."

"The beginning of the manuscript covers that time. When you and Braden were allegedly involved in the student uprising on the Carlyle campus." I swallowed a bite of tuna salad. I didn't expect it to be so delicious. I took another.

"*Does* it?" Cheryl sliced off a piece of cheddar.

"As I said, it was written by my dad, Jim Castle. Does that name mean anything to you?"

Cheryl shook her head slowly. "No. Sorry, I don't recognize the name."

"I'm not sure how my dad found out so much about Braden. Could be they met somewhere along the way and Braden told him his story. Dad never talked about his past."

"So, what exactly does your dad say about Braden … about us?"

"That you both were involved in student protests at Carlyle, and that you were very much in love."

She couldn't hold back the smile.

"There's a description of the bombing of the ROTC building in the spring of 1970 and how Braden set it off. Did that actually happen?"

"Oh yes. We were both politically active back then. It was a volatile time. But why is that of any interest to you, Nick?"

"Well, I think it's a fascinating story. I'm considering using my dad's account as the basis for a novel about Braden

262

Delaney—about what happened around the time of the bombing and in the years after he escaped capture."

She gasped, hand to her heart. "This manuscript … it tells you about what happened to Braden … *after* he had to go on the run?"

I nodded. "It does, but I'm not sure how much of it is true. I mean, my dad could have made up a lot of the story."

She picked up her fork, set it back down.

I waited, watched her bite her lower lip to try to keep it from trembling. Didn't work.

She leaned against the back of the couch, looked over at me. "Please, I'd love to hear about it anyway."

"Short version. Braden made it to the Oregon coast. He managed to escape aboard a drug smuggler's boat to El Salvador, where he was robbed of everything and left for dead."

Cheryl's eyes widened.

"But a Salvadoran family helped him recover, and from there he escaped into Honduras, where he lived for almost a decade as a migrant worker. Eventually, he had to escape Honduras … one step ahead of the authorities."

"So, he was always on the run." She sniffed, dabbed her nose with a linen napkin.

"Mostly, yeah. After he fled Honduras, he spent several years in Mexico before sneaking back into the United States with a new identity. The story ends there. He'd lived in exile more than fifteen years after he left Sinclair."

She stared past me, her eyes blank. I could barely hear her say, "I always hoped he got away. I never heard anything about him being caught." She eased out a sigh. "All these years I was afraid he died all alone somewhere."

"Wait. I heard Braden made it back to Sinclair eventually."

She refocused on me, blinked. "What? Does the manuscript say he returned here?"

"Well, no. But I talked with Groovy Greg, and he implied that you and Braden had reunited."

She rolled her eyes. "I wouldn't put much stock in anything that old geezer says." She looked away. "The truth is, I never saw Braden again."

"Oh my God, I'm so sorry. I must have misinterpreted …"

She patted the corner of her eye with her napkin.

I gave her a moment. Hell, I needed one myself. My house of cards could be about to collapse right in front of me. I clutched my hands together to keep them from shaking.

Eventually, Cheryl sucked in a ragged breath, tried to smile. "But you're more interested in the time Braden and I were together."

"Um, yeah. I'd like to see if what actually happened jibes with what I've read." I pulled a pad from my jacket pocket. "Mind if I take a few notes?"

"Of course not." She tapped her chin with the tips of her long fingers. "Back then, I was the quintessential uppity Black woman. I had the biggest, boldest Afro you ever saw." She held her hands about two feet apart on either side of her head. "Like Angela Davis." She offered a crooked smile. "You probably don't even know who that is."

"I've seen her picture."

"Then you know what I'm talking about. I even dressed in dashikis a lot of the time. Of course, I was pretty easy to spot on campus, since there was only a handful of black folk at Carlyle in those days, and I was one of the few who wasn't there on an athletic scholarship. Even though the Civil Rights Act outlawed racial discrimination, we were still treated with hatred and violence pretty much everywhere."

"I can't begin to imagine what that was like."

She looked at me, expressionless. "No, Nick, you can't. But you aren't expected to. It's a different world now. Discrimination today is usually handled in much subtler ways."

She dug her manicured nails into the palm of her right hand, exhaled, then gently lowered her hands to her lap. "Sorry. I didn't mean to get us off track. We were talking about the bombing of the ROTC building at Carlyle."

"Yeah. It was in the spring, right? Around the time of the Kent State shootings?"

"Yes, right after that." She squeezed her eyes shut. "Like so many college students back then, Braden and I were convinced it was morally wrong for the government to send troops to Vietnam. And it was obvious the U.S. was losing, despite the claims on TV each night that America was winning the body count contest."

"We read a little bit about that in school, and Dad alluded to what it was like in his manuscript. But he and I never really talked about it much."

"Well, suffice it to say the authorities turned our peaceful protests into a bloodbath. Students were being shot and killed all across the country, all within a couple of weeks. It honestly felt like we were under attack by our own government. Nixon claimed the antiwar protests were the work of a few crazed student radicals. 'Bums' he called us." She eased out a breath through clenched teeth.

I picked up my cup, took a sip.

"Braden and I formed a small, secret group of Carlyle students who vowed to show the world we weren't going to let the feds bully us. Braden's setting off that explosion was absolutely a heroic act." She pushed her plate aside and stood.

I started to rise, but she gestured for me to stay put. "I think better when I move around a little." She began to wander the room. I noticed she'd slipped out of her shoes. Her socks were bright yellow with black stripes. Somehow perfect for her.

She ran the back of her hand through the leaves of the philodendron in the corner. It was a lot bigger than the one we had at Book Castle.

"After the bombing, we both knew Braden was going to have to lie low for a while."

She paused in front of the picture window and peered out at Lake Washington, her back to me. "Then, right after he went on the run, they found that girl's body. The authorities claimed the bombing was no more than an attempt to cover up a murder. The bastards."

She paced again. "Braden didn't even know that girl was in the building. He would never have set off the bomb if he thought anyone would be hurt. Beneath all of his impassioned rhetoric, Braden was kind and gentle at heart. That didn't matter to the authorities. The media jumped at the chance to turn him into a crazed killer." She clenched her hands into tight fists.

"Yeah, Dad's version says the killing of the girl was totally an accident."

She relaxed her hands and turned back to me. "No, it was murder all right. But Braden wasn't the killer. The murderer was a grad student named Will Lafferty. He was *one* of us, so Lafferty knew about the plan to bomb the ROTC building. I guess he figured it was his chance to get rid of his pregnant girlfriend. Lafferty didn't get away with it, though. He's doing life in the state pen at Walla Walla."

This was new to me. I wrote it down.

She padded over to the piano and played her fingers silently along the top of the keys. "It's all a kind of ironic justice, I suppose. Lafferty was the one who ratted out Braden to the authorities, but *he* ended up in prison, while Braden lived a free man ... in exile."

I heard a catch in her voice.

"So, Braden was cleared of the murder, then?" I asked.

"Yes, he was exonerated of the murder charge. But if he was hiding out in another country he would never have known." She stared into space.

I took a sip of warm tea.

Studying her hands, she said, "We were so young then. I was nineteen and Braden had just turned twenty. Neither of us was looking for a relationship, but it didn't take long for us to fall in love. It was real, and it was deep."

"Oh, the manuscript makes that *very* clear."

She spun back to face me, eyes wide. "It *does*?" She beamed. "You know? Even after all these years, I still have a special place in my heart for Braden. I've been married twice, both times to fine men. But neither of those marriages lasted long. My fault." She stared into space. "Because even after all these years, I've never really stopped loving Braden." She pivoted back toward the window, but not before I saw her tears.

"I'm sorry. I didn't mean to upset you."

Without looking back at me, she waved away my concern. "Oh, I'm fine, Nick. But will you excuse me for a moment?" She turned back, forced a smile. "I'd like a minute to collect my thoughts."

I stood. "Sure, let's take a break. May I use your restroom?" She nodded toward the hallway. "First door on the left."

Chapter 35

When I returned, Cheryl was leaning forward on the piano bench, face in her palms.

I wasn't sure she realized I'd come back. I settled on the sofa, lifted the teapot. "Would you like more tea?"

She stood and returned to the couch. "Yes, thank you, Nick." She slumped onto the sofa across from me. "You have to understand that Braden didn't have a choice. He had to get away from Carlyle fast. I never heard from him again, but, honestly, though I hoped to … I really didn't expect to. We both knew that the feds would be monitoring me closely. And they did. They tapped my phone and followed me everywhere for nearly a year. They were tenacious."

I refilled our cups. "So, you're saying he never *really* abandoned you and the baby?"

"I know Brady still thinks he did. I've tried to explain it to him, but he's a bit hard-nosed. Takes after his mother, I suppose." She forced a smile.

I lifted my cup, took a sip.

"Braden didn't even know I was pregnant when he escaped. Neither did *I*. But I kept the baby because he was *our* baby. I knew it was all I'd ever have to remember him by."

She stared into the steam rising from her teacup. "If Braden had known he had a son, he would have tried to come back. And he surely would have been caught and sent to prison. Thank God he never found out."

I picked up a grape from the platter, examined it. "If you don't mind my asking, why didn't you get as far away from Sinclair as possible? This area must have been full of sad memories for you." I popped the grape into my mouth.

"I dropped out of college when I found out I was pregnant, but I stayed in the area because, even though Braden could never come back here, I figured any news of him would warrant at least a mention in the local paper, even after the story turned cold."

She raised the cup to her lips, hesitated. "Besides, a small town like Sinclair was a good, safe place to raise our son." She took a sip and set the cup back down on its saucer. "I grew up in Chicago, so I knew what life could be like in a big city— especially for young Black males. Still today, it's a harsh existence there. That's one of the reasons my parents sent me clear out to Carlyle. They didn't want me to associate with people they considered 'undesirables.' They made sure my speech and demeanor reflected a higher level of culture." She pantomimed air quotes for the last part of the sentence.

I nodded, returned to my notes. Maybe Cheryl would play a larger role in the novel than I'd thought. "What about your parents? Couldn't they help?"

"They could ... but they wouldn't." Cold eyes. "They were adamantly against me dating Braden from the start. They didn't think he was good enough for me. In their eyes, *no* one was. My father had become a rich man by serving as the token

Black in management for a huge investment firm. He succeeded because he avoided associating himself with anything that might piss off his White bosses. My parents expected me to follow the same path so I could have the finer things in life. I knew I already had the finest thing I could imagine … loving Braden. My relationship with him was the last straw for my parents."

She looked away, her lips a thin tight line. "They both died without ever seeing their only grandson. My father never forgave me, but my mother must have felt something. When she passed away a few years ago, she left me enough in her will to ensure I'll be able to live quite comfortably for the rest of my life. Nice, but much too late to help me when I needed it."

"You are an amazing woman, you know that?"

"You're *so* young, Nick." She sighed. "What I did with my life was no more than any good mother would do. I put my child first, and I did what I could to make his life happy. That's not amazing. That's just love."

"What a beautiful sentiment." I wrote it down, stole a look at my watch. I placed my hands at the edge of the couch, ready to push myself up. "I've really enjoyed spending time with you, Cheryl. But I should probably—"

She held up her hand. "Before you go, Nick, tell me about your dad. I'd like to get a sense of the man who chose to write down Braden's story."

I gritted my teeth, holding back a wave of emotion that caught me by surprise. "Dad died a month and a half ago. Prostate cancer."

Her hand flew up to her mouth. "Oh! I'm so sorry, Nick." Deep breath. "It has to be a terrible loss for you. You sure you're okay talking about him?"

My chest was so tight it hurt. "Yeah, I guess so. Um, he established Book Castle, our mom-and-pop bookstore in Shoat Valley. He's ... he *was* a big reader. He told me once he always wanted to write a novel. That's one of the reasons I'm serious about getting his story out there."

She looked me over, grinned. "I'm thinking he must have been a good-looking guy." Raised an eyebrow. "I mean judging by his son."

My cheeks burned.

"So, give me a mental picture of your dad?"

"Dad was tall, a little over six feet same as me, dark hair starting to thin and turn gray, and he'd developed just a hint of a paunch. I teased him about it, but he wasn't fat. I guess you could say he still looked like an athlete even into his sixties." I paused for a swallow of warm tea. "But he always had this great smile. It ... I don't know how to describe it exactly."

She closed her eyes and steepled her hands together in front of her chin. "I think I can picture it." She flicked a tear from the corner of her eye.

"Dad was able to make anyone feel better just by being in the same room with them. Everyone who knew him loved him."

"He was a special person." Cheryl seemed to be studying an invisible pattern somewhere off to her left.

"Yes, he was." I hesitated, thought about how to say it. "I guess you could say he lived every day to the fullest. I mean, in a small-town, small-life sort of way." I managed a weak

272

laugh. "Weird thing was, though, he didn't like to talk about his past. I don't know anything about my grandparents on Dad's side. It was almost … well, Mom thinks he suffered from some form of PTSD. She thinks something terrible must have happened to him when he was young. But that's just a guess." I dropped my gaze to the dishes on the coffee table. "And now we'll never know." My voice sounded tiny and woeful, even to me.

"Sweetie, a parent can't share everything with a child. There are many things children don't need to know." She winked. "Besides, we try to keep the illusion alive as long as we can that we're perfect. Kids find out soon enough that their parents are only human."

"Well, it certainly doesn't matter now." I recalled how upset I'd been at Dad when I suspected he'd concealed his true identity for all these years. Yes, I'd been childish and angry. And hurt. But damn it, Dad deserved better. He needed his son to grow the fuck up.

A hint of a smile tugged at the edges of Cheryl's mouth. "Your dad sounds wonderful."

"Yeah, he was. Friendly, humble, honest. Dad never put himself first. For someone who spent so much of his life in a small town, he understood people." I sucked in a breath to cover the quiver in my voice. "He was a great guy."

She bit her lower lip. "I'd say you were one lucky kid to have a father like him."

I fidgeted on the couch, looked into her sad eyes. "You know? Maybe it'd be best to leave the past buried. Maybe writing about you and Braden Delaney—even if I changed your names—would be too much an invasion of your privacy." I stood.

Cheryl rose in tandem with me, reached out, and rested her hand on my shoulder. "Write your novel, Nick. It could be a way to keep Braden alive forever. I'd like that. I think of him every day. And those memories will never fade away."

"Braden Delaney must have been a special guy to deserve the undying love of a woman like you, even after all these years."

Cheryl peered at me as if she were trying to see into my soul. "He was special, Nick. He surely was."

I squirmed and stole another look at my watch. "Here, let me help you with these dishes." I placed my plate and cup on the tea tray.

"Just leave them, Nick. I'll take care of it later. It'll give me something to do after you're gone … while I'm going through the photos of Braden in my mind."

I resolved to remember that line. What a way to describe memories.

"Nick, may I ask you a favor?"

"Sure. Anything."

"I'd love it if you would send me a copy of your novel when you've finished. It would give me a way to relive Braden's life after he escaped."

"Of course!" Forehead slap. Why hadn't I thought of that already? "Listen, if you like, I'll make a copy of Dad's manuscript and send *that* to you. So, you won't have to wait for me to get around to grinding out the novel and trying to convince someone to publish it."

She clasped her hands together like a schoolgirl. "Oh, that would be wonderful, Nick. It would mean so much to me. More than you could possibly know." Behind her, over the lake, the sun peeked out from a cloud to backlight her. I was taken again by the grace and elegance of Cheryl Stevens.

"Hold on." She headed down the hall out of sight.

She returned with a small manila envelope and handed it to me.

I glanced at it. Her mailing address was pre-printed in the upper left, and she'd written her email and phone number below it. "I promise, I'll send it to you, Cheryl. I'll take care of it as soon as I get back home." I held out my hand.

She stared at my hand, chuckled. "I'd rather give you a hug." She pulled me into her embrace and squeezed me tight. I thought I could feel her trembling against me. Was she sobbing? I kept up my side of the hug until she finally set me free.

"I'll walk you out." She turned away. If she'd been crying, she didn't want me to see it.

Cheryl stood in her doorway, and I felt her watching me make my way down the hall to the elevator.

As the doors began to open, I swung back around and waved goodbye.

She managed to smile through the flowing tears, just before she slipped back inside.

I swallowed the lump in my throat. I hadn't meant to upset her. I remembered Brady's warning, but I couldn't be sure if hers were tears of sadness or tears of joy at being able to relive some lost moments with the one great love of her life.

As I approached my car, I tried to fold the envelope in half to slip it into my jacket pocket, but it resisted. It wasn't empty. I reached inside and eased out an old photo. On the back, Cheryl had written, "Braden and me. Spring 1970." I flipped it over. Two people beamed back at me—Cheryl, with her huge Afro, and a cocky-looking young white guy with his arm around her.

I froze. Too dizzy to take another step, I braced myself against the car. When I finally caught my breath, I studied the photo again.

Young Braden Delaney looked exactly like me.

Chapter 36

I dropped into the front seat like a 193-pound bag of rocks and stared into the fog where the dashboard used to be.

A familiar ache in my chest told me I was about to start bawling, but tears wouldn't come. I tried to scream, but I didn't have the breath. I was so angry I wanted to punch someone. Anyone. Dad? Cheryl? Of course not. Maybe.

Cheryl had known from the second she first saw me that Dad was Braden Delaney. Damn it! I'd trusted her, and she'd stomped all over that trust. Why did she wait until the last goddamn second to let me know the truth? Had she been secretly laughing at me the whole time? I must have looked like a fucking idiot. Why did she have to tell me at *all*? Her stringing me along felt like pure maliciousness. But face it, Cheryl wasn't a malicious woman. Truth was, I'd liked her, respected her. Still did.

I drove my fist into my palm. If anybody needed punching, it was *me*. I'd never felt so stupid. There was simply no way Dad could have known all those details about Braden Delaney unless he experienced them himself. If this manuscript had been an attempt at a novel, why keep it a secret until after his death? The truth had been staring me in the face the whole damn time, but I'd done everything I could to avoid it.

Shouldn't have been that hard to see. Unless you happened to be a complete *moron*.

Okay, maybe I wasn't a moron, but what exactly *was* I? When I left Shoat Valley I knew for sure who I was—a son whose main goal in life was to emulate the man he loved and admired. But everything was different now.

The digital clock on the dashboard came into focus: 2:33 p.m. Shit. Just enough time to get to the airport to pick up Sophie, if I hurried. With Sophie, I *knew* who I was. I needed to focus on that. I started the car and aimed it at SeaTac.

As soon as she spotted me, Sophie raced over, dropped her carry-on, and leaped into a hug. When I finally let go, she studied me.

"Are you all right, Nick? Did something happen with the old lady?"

"It's all better now you're here." I lifted her chin, and we kissed.

She stepped back and beamed at me. It sent a rush of emotion all the way down to my toes.

I picked up her carry-on, and we rode a tram and a couple of escalators to the baggage carousel. As soon as she spotted hers, I grabbed it, released the handle, and pulled it behind me as we headed out of the terminal, her arm in mine.

Once I'd maneuvered the Prius through the airport maze, I had a straight shot on the commute-crowded freeway to downtown. She was ecstatic about the beauty of Seattle, how much fun we were going to have during the long Memorial Day weekend playing tourist at the Space Needle, Pike Place Market, and all the other sites we'd heard of but had never seen in person. But my contribution to the conversation consisted mostly of mumbled responses to her enthusiasm.

Small talk with Sophie had been so easy until now. What the hell was the matter with me? This was Sophie for Christ's sake! Come on, I got this. Right?

She glanced over at me. "Okay, mister, out with it. Who are you, and what have you done with the sweet, fun guy I've grown so fond of?"

I stiffened, a burglar nabbed in the act. My smile felt more like a grimace. "Don't worry. I'm still the same guy. Got blindsided is all."

Sophie gave my arm a squeeze. "Wanna talk about it? For someone who's been accused of never knowing when to shut up, I can be a pretty good listener."

Yes, Cheryl had tossed an emotional hand grenade into my life, but I knew that Sophie would hear me and understand—maybe more than I did.

"Know what? I think you may be the only one I *can* talk to about it. But it's a long story. Maybe after we get settled in."

◆ ◆ ◆

"I love this!" Sophie danced through our spacious room at the Mayflower Park. "It's way better than some fancy-schmancy modern hotel where even the furniture seems snooty."

I managed a laugh, disregarding the dark cloud still hanging over me. "Yeah, they call it Queen Anne style." I gestured to the promotional literature artfully arranged on the

279

desk. I'd skimmed some of it last night, but it hadn't been much of a distraction.

She ran her fingers along the smooth surface of the antique armoire. "It's almost as if we've been transported back in time, you know?" She twirled back to me. "Like our being here has a kind of, I dunno, historical significance?" Her blue eyes gleamed.

"Well, the room's a lot more significant … and more *stylish* now that you're in it." I shrugged. "Last night it was just a place to sleep."

She glided over and kissed me on the cheek. "You are *such* a smooth talker, Nick Castle." She stepped back. "But I've been traveling for almost six hours. I promise I'll be a lot more stylish, maybe even more significant, after a shower."

As I watched Sophie head off to the bathroom, a now-familiar warm wave flowed through my body, and I knew. I was falling in love with her. There, I said it. And if I'd never started this journey, we would've never met. She was wonderful, maybe even perfect for me. But did I have what it took to keep up with a strong, smart, independent woman like Sophie Cole?

Even if I was up to the task, did we honestly have a shot at a future together? Given her mother's condition, Sophie couldn't leave Port Orford. And, no way I could abandon Mom and Shelby so soon after we lost Dad. Not to mention, I had a bookstore to run. I was stuck in Shoat Valley for the foreseeable future.

And what was I going to do about Chelsea? She had plans for us—long-term plans—and she had every right to those expectations. But something had always been missing in our relationship. Whatever that something was, I'd found it with

Sophie. Chelsea deserved an explanation, but I wasn't sure I could come up with one that wouldn't hurt her … deeply.

I knew what Dad would say—what Dad *did* say. I could still hear his voice like it was yesterday: "When you find someone you love, *really* love, promise me you won't walk away. If you do, you might never have another chance."

At the time, I hadn't understood he was giving me much more than good advice. Now I knew he was talking from firsthand experience. Even though he truly loved Mom, Dad had been secretly lamenting the loss of his first love, Cheryl Stevens. It was that powerful.

I'd promised him that *I* wouldn't walk away. And I meant to do everything I could to keep that promise—despite the significant roadblocks Sophie and I would have to face along the way.

Besides, right now I had something more immediate in mind. I shed my clothes and surprised Sophie in the shower.

Chapter 37

Later, wrapped in matching, fluffy white hotel robes, we lounged on the floor, a room-service feast spread out in front of us like a catered picnic, the room lit only by the muted TV screen and a bedside lamp. And we talked. First, I admitted my ruse about researching a novel, then I filled her in.

"As you know my dad passed away … recently."

Sophie nodded, her eyes sympathetic.

"But you *don't* know that a few months before he died, Dad gave me an envelope, with instructions not to open it until after he was gone. And that led me to a handwritten journal, which I assumed was Dad's attempt to write a novel."

I told her everything. The manuscript narrative. How I translated the name of "Diego Alcázar" to "James Castle," and began to suspect it might not be a novel at all. I went through everything that had happened since. I admitted to being in denial until my resolve finally unraveled when Cheryl Stevens gave me an old photo. I showed it to Sophie, wiped my eyes with the sleeve of my robe.

She looked at the picture, then back to me, her eyes wide.

Now, with Sophie sitting across from me, I felt as if the plug had been pulled on all my pent-up vitriol and pain. It was easier to breathe. It was a start.

"But your journey isn't over yet, is it?" Sophie handed me a napkin.

I shook my head, blotted my eyes. Then I leaned back against the edge of the bed. "I've always loved being a chip off the old Jim Castle block. It defined me. I was a proud replica. But now that the old block has crumbled, where the hell does that leave the chip?"

Sophie reached over and took my hand in hers.

I squeezed back. "And there's a lot more at stake than just me. I mean, do I tell Mom what I've discovered? Or my sister, Shelby? What would that do to our family?" I heard the rising shrillness in my voice, stopped, looked over at Sophie.

She slid over next to me and refilled our wine glasses. "I wouldn't presume to tell you what you should do, even if I knew. It's your call, Nick. But your dad said that whatever decision you make would be the right one, didn't he?"

"Yes, he did." Remembering that took some pressure off, but it didn't give me a clue about how to *make* that right decision.

"So, you can't go wrong whatever you decide. At least not in your dad's opinion." She glanced up as if the ceiling of our room on the seventh floor were close enough to heaven to make her point.

"I know. You're right. But I'm not sure that makes it any easier. People could be hurt if I screw it up."

She stood. "My advice? Sleep on it. I'm willing to bet, in the morning, you'll have a better handle on what you should

283

do—and what you *shouldn't* do." She reached down and took my hand.

I rose and pulled her close. "I hope you're right, Babe. Anyway, I'm tired of talking." I tipped my head toward the bed.

Sophie grinned, reached down, undid the belt on my robe, and slipped it off my shoulders. Hers joined mine on the floor.

We eased into an embrace and shared a kiss. That kiss lit the fuse that detonated built-up emotions inside both of us. We gave in to our need for each other, until we finally nestled together, tangled in the sheets of our Queen Anne-style bed.

♦　♦　♦

We'd planned to get out early and spend the day exploring Seattle's waterfront. Good plan. But it almost ten when we stepped out of the Starbucks across the street from our hotel with two chocolate croissants and a couple of double cappuccinos. The hotel concierge had given us a street map and drawn the route to the famous Pike Place Market. We did the half-mile trek on foot. We spent almost two hours browsing the shops, watching giant salmon being tossed around at the fish market, looking over the exotic selections of produce— generally oohing, aahing, and laughing like a couple of tourists on a honeymoon.

I did my best to embrace the moment, and I contributed to the enthusiasm for the most part. When I focused on Sophie, it was easy. But crouching in the back of my brain was the task still ahead of me. What was the right thing to do now that I knew the truth about Dad?

Carrying a tote bag with our purchases—a couple of Pike Place T-shirts, and lots of fruit and snacks—we crossed the street to check out the stalls and shops outside the market. I was once again lost in thought. I *got* why Cheryl waited to tell me the truth. She had me spell out Dad's virtues as a father and mentor ... as a human being. So *that* would be the freshest image in my mind when she gave me the photo.

"Earth to Nick." Sophie patted my arm to rouse me, as we crossed the street to Beecher's Handmade Cheese.

"What?" Sheepish grin. "Sorry, I was just thinking about something."

"I just asked you if you were getting hungry. It's almost one o'clock."

"You know? I am getting a little peckish."

We stepped inside, returned the welcoming smile from the round-faced, gray-haired guy at the counter. He gestured to the variety of cheeses on display. "You gotta try some of our cheeses. We make them right here in the shop."

We sampled several. In the end, I bought a couple of seven-ounce triangles of New Woman. Both Sophie and I loved its Jamaican jerk spices.

As we finished the transaction, Sophie asked the counterperson, "Any recommendations for lunch?"

"What kind of food do you kids have in mind?"

We looked at each other, grinned. "Seafood," we answered in unison.

He chuckled. "Well, you're in the perfect spot for that. I'm guessing you're new to Seattle, which means you've never eaten at Ivar's Acres of Clams."

"I think I've heard the name," I said.

"Yeah, probably have. Pretty famous. Started here back in the thirties."

"Sounds great," Sophie said. "How do we get there?"

"It's a bit of a walk from here, but it's worth it. Just a pleasant stroll along Alaskan Way on the waterfront. Just keep goin' 'til you get to Ivar's. Can't miss it."

Took us forty-five minutes to get to the restaurant, mostly because we were in and out of nearly every shop along the way.

♦ ♦ ♦

Sitting on the outside deck at Ivar's, we enjoyed a breathtaking view of Puget Sound. Sophie had the fresh grilled Alaska salmon; I had Ivar's world-famous fish and chips. We traded bites back and forth until both plates were empty. So were our wine glasses, so I ordered another round.

On the way out I bought Sophie a pair of socks that featured the slogan: "Keep Clam." Ivar's catchphrase.

We paused outside the restaurant and looked back down Alaskan Way.

"So, should I get us a cab? Or do you feel like walking back to the hotel?" I asked.

"Oh, let's walk." She smiled. "There's so much more to see along the way."

"Makes sense to retrace our tracks, then. Don't wanna get lost on our way back."

"Works for me." Sophie took a couple of steps down the sidewalk, then pivoted back.

I hadn't moved. I was transfixed by a dad carrying a toddler on his shoulders, the child giggling and the dad laughing right along with him. I've made those giggles, and I've heard those laughs. But, for me, those times were gone forever. And my memories of them were now tainted. Shit.

Sophie followed my gaze, returned to my side. We watched until the dad and son entered a shop twenty feet in front of us. She took me in her arms. "Good memories, huh?"

I held her tight. "Yeah. I have nothing but wonderful memories of the Dad I knew. But I still can't get my head around the fact he's also Braden Delaney—someone I *never* knew."

"You'll work it out, Babe," she whispered against my chest.

I released her. "I'm counting on you being right." I took her arm in mine. "Okay, then let's hoof it back to the hotel and try to keep from exploring every cute shop along the way."

She grinned. "Hmm, I suppose we can *try*."

◆　◆　◆

By the time we made it back to the room, it was 5:30. I stretched. "I don't feel much like dinner yet. Still full from lunch."

Sophie kicked off her sandals and plopped down on the edge of the bed. "What I need right now isn't food." She dropped back onto the mattress. "After all that exploring … and all that walking, I think we've earned a nap."

"Great idea." I grinned. "And maybe we can catch a little sleep, too."

Turned out we were more exhausted than we thought. It was already getting dark when we finally awoke at 7:45. We

287

had a late dinner and a bottle of Cabernet Sauvignon at the hotel restaurant. By 9:30 we were back in bed for the night.

Chapter 38

According to the bedside clock it was just after midnight when I eased out of Sophie's warm embrace and slipped into my robe. I stepped over to the window, pulled open the drapes enough to gaze out upon the Seattle skyline just visible above the low fog, the Space Needle piercing through it in the distance.

"What would you tell your dad if he were here right now?"

I twisted around at the sound of Sophie's voice to see her wrapped in the sheet, sitting up on the bed, her knees pulled up to her chin. Adorably sexy.

She reached over and turned on the nightstand light. "It might help if you told him how you feel."

"What? You mean *now*? He's not even ... he's gone."

"Try it anyway. Trust me, I have a bachelor of arts in psychology."

My grin matched hers. "Well, you're the expert." I turned back to the window. "Gotta tell you, this feels weird, though."

"At first it does, but it'll get easier."

With the light behind me, Seattle faded into the background. My own image looked back at me. And, as always, I could see Dad's features. And from now on, I'd always see Braden Delaney.

Deep breath. "I miss you, Dad. A lot." I felt my throat tighten. "I know why you needed to keep your secret, but why did you have to dump it all on me? Damn it, I've spent my whole life trying to be just like you." I sucked in a ragged breath. "Like the person I *thought* you were. Now that you've turned out to be someone else … I-I don't know who *I* am anymore." I looked away, ran my fingers through my hair.

"You're doing great, Nick." Sophie stepped up beside me, handed me the photo Cheryl had given me. "Maybe this will help."

I set the photo on the windowsill, looked back up at the sad-eyed image before me. I saw no anger, no mind-crushing doubt. Instead, my image seemed full of pride. And responsibility. The dad I knew and the person he was early in his life were only memories. I was left to carry on … and live up to Dad's legacy.

"You'll always be the father I loved, looked up to. You, Mom, Shelby, and I had a wonderful life together. You were our rock. But now I know you were something more than that."

I paused, exhaled. Then I felt a smile forming deep inside me. "I didn't handle the truth well when I first learned about your real identity. It felt like a slap in the face. But I understand now." I paused, searched for the right words. "It's not about me. It's about you. You lost all those years in exile, but you spent the rest of your life making up for that loss. From where I stand, you did a damn good job of it." I hesitated. "I didn't think I

290

could have any greater respect for you than I did when we were together, but I do now. I'm prouder than ever to be your son."

I waited until I could speak through the lump in my throat. "You wanted *me* to know your real story all along. Otherwise, why leave your manu … *journal* for my eyes only? I just wish I'd handled it better … like a son who'd truly absorbed the life lessons his father taught him." I turned to the side, used the back of my hand to wipe my eyes. My throat felt raw enough to bleed.

Sophie, the mind reader, came up behind me with a bottle of water from the in-room fridge. "Take your time, Nick. I know this is tough."

I nodded my thanks, took a long drink. Fighting back the tears, I faced the window. "I miss you so much. Always will. And I hope someday to be the kind of father for my children that you've been for Shelby and me… and the kind of husband you've always been for Mom."

I was spent. I slumped forward, wiped my sweaty palms on the robe, rested them on the cool windowsill. Then I freed the pent-up tears.

Sophie handed me a box of tissues and wrapped her arms around me from behind.

I wiped my eyes, squinted through my reflection at the Seattle skyline again. The fog had all but dissipated now, and it must have rained sometime in the night. Everything looked washed clean.

She released me from her embrace. "You've made your decision, haven't you?"

I turned to face her. "Maybe. I mean, I *think* I have. Dad meant for me to make the call whether or not I'd tell Mom and Shelby about his past. Not that easy."

She nodded, kept silent.

"I'll sit Shelby down and tell her the whole story. She deserves to know about Braden Delaney… and about Cheryl, our half-brother Brady and our brand-new nephew. All of it. I'll find the right opportunity once she gets over Dad being gone. Nobody's mourning period is over yet."

"And?" Sophie raised an eyebrow.

"Shelby and I can decide together if we want to tell Mom. But what possible good would come from revealing all this to her? She doesn't need to know Dad's secret past, to be told there was—still is—another woman in Dad's life. It's obvious Mom is content with her memories of the life we all shared in Shoat Valley; she's never wanted anything more than that. She knows how much Dad loved her. That's enough."

"Don't underestimate your mom. She may know more than you realize. And it's not going to be easy to keep this from her."

"It might require some clever tap dancing, but if Dad could manage it all those years, so can Shelby and I." I released a breath I didn't realize I was hanging on to.

"*I'd* want to know about my husband's past." Sophie paused, looked me in the eye. "I imagine this revelation of Braden Delaney has been a lot tougher on you than it will be for your mom and Shelby."

We padded over to the bed, climbed aboard, and sat together, our backs against the headboard.

I took her hand in mine. "You're probably right. Mom and Shelby don't have their self-image … their whole identity at stake like I did. Like I *thought* I did."

"Just sayin'. Your dad's past had *nothing* to do with his marriage to your mom or your life together."

"Well, when you put it that way, it makes sense to tell Mom the whole story … including Cheryl, Brady, and the new little guy. Yeah, you're right. She'd want to know. Even if the baby won't officially be related to her, he's another part of Dad's legacy."

Sophie rubbed my shoulder through the robe.

"Another lesson learned," I said. "Been a lot of those lately."

She looked me in the eye, waiting.

"Okay, how 'bout this for a lesson learned? I never expected finding out the truth about Dad's past would give me a new sense of *myself.*"

She studied me in mock seriousness. "I'm not seeing a difference."

I laughed. "Well, for one thing, I'm more than merely a mirror image of Jim Castle." I shrugged. "I dunno. I guess I feel a hell of a lot older and wiser than the kid who left Shoat Valley a few days ago." I took in a deep breath, let it out. "From this point on, Nick Castle is his own man. It's a good feeling."

Sophie shifted around and pulled me into a hug, rested her head on my chest. "So, what happens next?"

"Tomorrow I'm going to photocopy the journal and deliver it to Cheryl in person. Dad's story will mean as much to her as it did to me. Probably even more. I'd like to remain a part of her life." I paused, stared straight ahead.

293

Then I broke into a broad smile, my eyes grew wide. "Damn! Blows my mind that I have a half brother, a sister-in-law, and soon I'll have a nephew. Brady might be angry that his father was alive all these years and never contacted them. But Dad's journal explains why, and I think Cheryl can make Brady understand."

Sophie shot me a wry grin.

"What?"

"Just imagining Thanksgiving dinner at the Castles' with the whole extended family sitting around the table. Might be just a bit awkward."

I laughed. "Yeah, it might be… at first, anyway."

"And you really *are* going to write that alleged novel after all, aren't you?"

I shrugged. "Don't know if I'm up to the task, but I wanna give it a shot. Doesn't have to be a bestseller, but I need to tell Dad's story. I owe it to him."

Sophie's eyes lit up. "You know? If you write your dad's experience as a novel, it could be a way to bridge the topic with Shelby and your mom."

I looked at her, a smile forcing its way through. "You're a genius! Once they know the story, then I can lift the veil, tell them who it's really about."

"I think it's all gonna turn out just fine for everyone, Babe." She kissed me on the cheek.

I took her face in my hands. "But what do you say we take a break from Braden Delaney and Jim Castle for a while. After we drop off a copy of the journal with Cheryl, and I thank her for opening my eyes, I want to spend the rest of the weekend concentrating on Sophie Cole."

"Only the weekend?" She affected a passable pout.

"I'm confident we can make the right decision about *that*, too."

Sophie snuggled against me, and I held her tight. I knew I'd never walk away from her.

And I didn't need Dad to tell me.

About the Author

Mark Scott Piper has been writing professionally his entire adult life. He holds an M.A and a Ph.D. in English from the University of Oregon, and he taught literature and writing at the college level for several years.

Mark's bookshelves are overflowing. Among his favorites are Christopher Moore, John Irving, Barbara Kingsolver, Stephen Crane, William Faulkner, and Anne Lamott—all of whom successfully conspire to keep him humble.

His debut novel, *You Wish*, earned first-place gold in the 2019 American Eagle Book Awards. His short stories have appeared in *Short Story America*, *The California Writers Club Literary Review*, and a wide range of online literary magazines.

If you enjoyed *The Old Block*—or any novel by an independent author—please take a moment to post a brief review on Amazon, Goodreads, or elsewhere. You don't need to write an essay, and no one will be grading your work. On Amazon, reviews can be the difference between success and failure for independent authors.

For the latest information visit www.markpiper.net. You can email him at mark@markpiper.net

About *You Wish*

Mark Scott Piper's debut novel, *You Wish*, earned **first-place gold from 2019 American Eagle Book Awards.**

Imagine you are granted three wishes—and your second wish is captured by a television news crew and broadcast across the globe. Now the whole world knows you can wish for absolutely anything, and *it will come true*. Now imagine you're fourteen years old.

Jake Parker is about to finish the freshman year of what's shaping up to be a mediocre high school career. He's a late bloomer. His family is living hand-to-mouth. And worst of all, he's a nobody—until he discovers an ancient ship's lantern. With everyone on the planet watching to see what Jake's final wish will be, he becomes an instant media darling, and his social status at school skyrockets. That's the good news.

The bad news is pressure is bearing down on Jake from family, public opinion, the media, government agents, and crooked politicians as he struggles to come up with a final wish that will truly help mankind. But if he's going to pull that off, he has to outsmart them all.

What readers are saying about *You Wish*

"You Wish is a page-turner that'll make you wish for more."

"… a wonderfully conceived piece of fiction."

"What a great movie this would make. Highly recommended."

"What a fun ride!"

"Few writers can make the magical, the unbelievable come alive and turn it into reality, but Piper has done exactly that."

"Overall, this is an excellent story; well told, with heart and morality and a sense of good overcoming bad. Good story, great writing!"

"*You Wish* is a page-turner that'll make you wish for more."

www.ingramcontent.com/pod-product-compliance
Lightning Source LLC
Chambersburg PA
CBHW021503240626
47154CB00002B/476